The Koldest Kill

BY

SILVER RAY

The Koldest Kill

ISBN-13: 978-1508811176
ISBN-10: 1508811172

Cover design by CoverMe Designs
Edited by Gloria Palmer
Proofread & Typeset by Gloria Palmer

Published by:
Emperial Publishing
P.O. Box 211194
Detroit, MI 48221-1194
(313) 449-8543

Email: tonja@emperialpublishing.com
Website: www.emperialpublishing.com
First printing March 2015

Acknowledgements

I always have to thank God for He is the reason I am who and what I am. I thank my family for loving me at all times. I love you all. I have to thank my husband because he puts up with every emotion, tantrum, good days and bad days—he stays right by my side. I love you forever, Billy D. To my children, you all keep me going. When I'm sick and feel like I can't work, I think of you, and I get up and go to work. I want you all to have all your needs and wants. You guys are my life and I can't picture my life without you in it. Mommy loves you—Adena, Jaelin, Jniyah, and our precious baby girl Jya.

To my girl, Kisha, thank you so much for being my voice of reason. You are always real when it comes to our friendship. We are and will always be the B, the F, and the F. The first woman I ever called best friend, Zetar, you mean the world to me. I am so proud of the woman you've become. Keep up the good work.

Mom and Dad, I love you. To my Grammy, you are my heart, and I love you with all of it. To my Grandma B, we have come so far and we are now so close. Thank you for all the talks and good food. I love you.

To my right-hand woman, Ray, you know what it is—cousins by blood, sisters by love. To my niece KK, Auntie loves you and you know it. You are a strong little girl who will grow to be a strong woman. Keep shooting that ball; you have that fire. To my nephew J'Allen, a.k.a. Duke, I love you so much. Keep singing; you have the voice to make the world fall in love. To my little brothers, Dquan and Oshay, I love you both. Auntie Shelia, down there in VA, I love you.

I have a couple of people I must give a shout out. Cece, thank you for being my little reader. You kept me motivated. Every time you said this book is good, it made me push harder. Thanks, my poo.

To you, Raymond, thanks for being a hater. Yes, my haters are my motivators . . . I just rolled my eyes real hard. To Tonja, thank you for showing me love at all times. You are always here for me; even when you're working, you take the time to help me. I love you, girl. You're the best that ever did it. To my favorite Aunties, Shelley and Yolanda, I love you. R.I.H. my dear brother, Rev. James Mitchell. I love you. I bleed ink and write stories that make you think.

The Koldest Kill

Introduction

I was born and raised in Detroit, Michigan. I have three brothers and one sister. Raised on the westside in the Joy Road and Livernois area, my family was well known. My mother had a large family, six brothers and five sisters. They were known as the dozens; my uncles were off the chain. They caused all kinds of trouble through the hood. All of them sold drugs. Money wasn't a problem at all. My mom's sisters were either hoes or dope girls as well.

My mom was different; she wasn't a hoe or dealer. She went to school, graduated, and got a job at the hospital in housekeeping. Pay wasn't top dollar but it was working for her. Her goal was to get out of my grammy's house and move far away from the madness. My mom always had big dreams. She wanted the best for herself. All was well . . . until she met my father.

My father's name was Jaycion Jimerson. He was the big dope man in my mom's hood. The very things my mom was running from found her anyway. She met him in the hospital. She had to clean the rooms on his floor of the hospital. He was in the hospital with seven gunshots to the body. He watched my mother on a daily basis clean his room. When he was able to finally speak, he began to converse with her on the regular. The rest is history.

He treated her like a queen. Of course, in the beginning, he hid who he really was from her. He received disability due to his gunshot injuries, so my mother believed that's how they stayed on top. So naïve, she didn't know she was married to the biggest dope dealer in Detroit. Not only was he the dope man, he was a pimp as well. He never tried to pimp her out, but she didn't approve of his behavior once she learned his real profession. This began to cause problems in the marriage.

My mother tried to leave then found out she was pregnant. This forced her back into my dad's arms, and when their first son was born, they decided to stay together. Dad promised to get rid of the hoes, but he refused to leave the dope game. Things were fine for a while, but my father never changed. While on baby number three, my mom found out about his bottom-bitch being pregnant too. Mom had just gotten laid off her job of fifteen years, so she felt like she had no choice but to stay.

Weak and under my father's love spell, things just kept getting worse. On baby number five—me—my father began to beat my mom. For any and everything. He wanted her to fear him and she did. After giving birth to me, my mother went into a deep depression and she stopped caring. My brothers were all grown and in the streets, and my sister had run away because of my father's strict rules and beatings. I was left alone. I lived in that house terrified of my father. I watched him beat my mother on a daily basis. Hell, if there was a day he didn't hit her, it was only because he didn't come home that night. I would hide in my closet so afraid, thinking one day I would grow big enough to protect my mother.

That day finally came.

My mother and I were having dinner when my father came in drunk. We were laughing and talking, enjoying one another's company. My father had been gone for three days and we thought he wasn't coming back. We didn't call him or look for him. I was eleven years old and stood five-foot-four. I was frail but I thought I was ready. My dad demanded that my mother to come to the room and take care of him. For the first time *ever*, she refused. She told him she was spending time with me. He came out the room, grabbed her by her hair, and dragged her across the floor. She kicked and screamed as he punched her in her face and pulled her to the bedroom.

I sat at the table with tears streaming down my face. I cried so many tears there was a puddle on the table under my face. I heard my mom screaming and I got fed up. I jumped up, went to my room, and got my dad's gun out of my closet. I'd put it there just in case someone came to harm us when he was gone. He had so many guns, he'd never noticed the gun was missing. I knew how to shoot the gun because my dad would take me to the field and teach me how to shoot different types of guns. I checked the chamber to make sure the gun was loaded.

I burst in the room and yelled at my father to get off my mom. He was butt-ass naked because he'd decided to take sex from her although she'd said no. He looked back at me and noticed I had the gun.

"Girl, are you fuckin' crazy?!" my father said to me.

"No! I'M SICK OF YOU HURTING HER. SHE'S A GOOD WOMAN; ALWAYS HAS BEEN! YOU'RE JUST A CONTROLLING ASSHOLE!" I yelled.

Knowing there was no turning back, I had to kill his ass or I would end up dead. I saw my mom's face, wet from the tears and blood. Her shirt was ripped half off, exposing her breasts. He had ripped her panties off, so her pussy and ass were exposed as well. I saw the fear in her eyes and I saw a desperate woman crying out for help. The look in her eyes melted my heart.

I yelled, "HE WILL NEVER HURT YOU AGAIN!"

I pulled the trigger until the gun was just clicking. I shot my father seven times. I was numb. I dropped the gun and ran over to my mother. She was bleeding badly, and ran over and picked up the gun. She started wiping it off with a bloody shirt. Then she kept putting it in each of her hands, one at a time.

She called the police and said, "I just shot my husband."

I knew she was protecting me. I ran out the room crying because I didn't know what they would do to my mom. I didn't want her to take the blame. She'd lived in this prison for twenty years and I didn't want her to go to another prison. I begged my mom to tell the truth but she refused.

My mom was charged with second-degree murder and they gave her twenty years with the possibility of parole. My heart was broken.

I yelled out in the courtroom, "SHE DIDN'T DO IT! I DID! I DID IT! PLEASE DON'T TAKE MY MOM FROM ME."

I was escorted out the court, right to Child Services. The social worker I was assigned to asked me for phone numbers of close relatives; I didn't have any. I didn't know any of my mom's siblings, and my dad was from Mississippi, so I'd never met his people either. I ended up becoming a ward of the State.

At age eleven, you wouldn't normally be adopted; most people wanted young children. This strange-ass couple came to see me. I begged my worker to let me stay in the group home. She refused, and off I went with Mr. and Mrs. Morgan. They didn't have any children. I couldn't understand why they would want me and not a baby. I soon found out.

Mrs. Morgan, who was terrified of Mr. Morgan, reminded me of my mother. She did whatever that man told her to do, no questions asked. Once the adoption was final, I found out exactly why I was the one chosen. Late one night I was in the shower, getting cleaned up for bed, when I heard the door quietly open. I never heard it shut, so I peeked out the shower curtain, and there stood Mr. Morgan with his pants pulled down to his ankles, stroking his dick. I hurried and pulled the curtain shut.

I was so scared; I didn't know what to do. I called out for Mrs. Morgan. "MRS. MORGAN, WOULD YOU BRING ME A DRY TOWEL?" I peeked out the curtain and watched as Mr. Morgan eased out the bathroom. When Mrs. Morgan came in, she asked about the towel she noticed hanging on the back of the door. I just looked at her and the look in her eyes said she knew what she'd just saved me from.

She couldn't do much for me. I had to think about my next move. I knew one day he would catch me alone and I knew what he planned to do. That day came sooner than I thought. I came home from school and Mr. Morgan was home. Mrs. Morgan hadn't made it home from work, which was unusual. I walked in quietly and tried to ease up stairs. I went in my room and shut the door. Nervous as all get out, I sat on my bed, praying Mrs. Morgan would come home. I heard a car door, so I jumped up and looked out the window; it wasn't her. When I turned around, Mr. Morgan was standing there, naked.

"Come here, little girl; come sit on daddy's lap," he said with a creepy smile on his face.

"LEAVE ME ALONE! WHAT IS YOUR PROBLEM? YOU HAVE A WIFE!" I yelled, trying to stall.

"I don't want her. I want some new pussy, you know the kind that's never been touched—fresh, virgin pussy," he said as he approached me. He grabbed me and threw me on the bed. "If you cooperate, this will feel good to you as well," he said as he pulled my panties out from under my skirt with his free hand.

I knew I couldn't win a fight with him, but as he entered my small vagina, I knew I was going to kill him when this was over. Although it hurt like hell, I didn't cry, I took the pain. It was my motivation for murder.

He moaned and groaned, he even told me how good it felt. He asked if I liked how it felt. I pictured myself killing him, so I said yes. He took that statement all wrong. He began kissing me as if we were making love. He pulled himself out of me.

"Let me kiss it; I know it hurts. You're being a very good girl, baby," he said before he began to lick my vagina.

Although it felt pleasing to me, I still held on to my anger. I knew what he was doing to me was wrong. Once he'd finished, he got back on top of me and put his penis back inside my tiny vagina. I was in so much pain; he must have forgotten he was on top of a child. He was going so hard I couldn't control the tears that had begun to fall from my eyes. He opened my shirt and began sucking on my tiny little breasts.

He was so into what he was doing, moaning so loud, he didn't hear Mrs. Morgan come in. She softly pushed the door open and I could see a metal bat out the corner of my eye. She rushed in and hit him on top of his head. He was shocked by the blow and rolled off me. I jumped up and ran downstairs to the kitchen. I grabbed the biggest knife in the drawer. I ran back upstairs, and Mr. Morgan had Mrs. Morgan pinned to floor, beating her like a man. The rage in my eyes caused a flashback, and I saw my father beating my mom. I ran in, and with all my strength, I stabbed Mr. Morgan in his back. He was still trying to move, so I took my foot and kicked the knife deeper into his back, until his body lay still.

I looked at Mrs. Morgan, not sure how she felt. She told me she knew he was up to something. He'd told her to make several runs that made no sense. She said she'd thought about the bathroom incident, had done a U-turn, and headed back to the house. She called the police, and once again, like my mother, she told them she'd stabbed him when she arrived home and found him raping me. I guess there's something about being a mother that makes you protect your young. Although Mrs. Morgan and I didn't share blood, we shared something that bonded us for life.

When we went to trial, the jury found Mrs. Morgan innocent. They said the killing was justified. We walked out the courtroom, hand-in-hand. Mrs. Morgan looked me in my eyes and said, "You saved my life." I smiled at her and said, "I would do it again if I had to."

From that day on, we lived as a family, just her and I. Once the Morgans adopted me, my mother had no rights to me. Mrs. Morgan asked me if I wanted to start visiting my mother; of course I said yes. My mom and Mrs. Morgan became good friends. My mom was grateful Mrs. Morgan had protected me just as she had. We visited my mom twice a month, until they moved her out of state. The prison she was in was overcrowded, and because of her long sentence, she had to be moved. I was devastated, hurt, and confused, wondering why God had made my life so hard.

I tried to live as normal as possible. I made it to high school, where the girls hated me. I was so pretty they assumed I was stuck up. I was quiet and stayed to myself, only because, mentally, I was fucked up. I couldn't live as a normal child. I had two murders under my belt, a rape, no mother, and no father. Of course, I blamed myself for my mother being in prison. I thought about it constantly. I should have done some things different.

High school was so hard for me. All of the girls picked on me and all of the boys liked me. Because of my hatred for men, I stayed away from boys. I didn't mind being a loner; hell, everyone I loved got taken away, so I didn't want to get close to anybody. I studied hard and got straight A's. I was looking forward to going to college.

I wanted to cheer, so I was brave and tried out for the team. When I came to school the next day, my name wasn't on the list. I knew it was personal because I had done everything perfectly. Splits, toe touches, round offs, and the cheers they'd taught us—I'd done to a T. I'd made no mistakes and I was fed up. I approached the head cheerleader at lunchtime. Her name was Nikki.

"Excuse me; can you explain to me why I didn't make the cheer team?" I asked.

"Because I don't like you, and you're a fuckin' weirdo. Hey, ladies, this fuckin' weirdo wants to know why she didn't make it. Get the fuck out my face before I spit in your food!" she said as everyone laughed and pointed at me.

"Do it! I dare you, bitch!" I responded.

This bitch *spit* in my food. I dumped my food off my tray onto the floor and slapped that bitch with the tray so hard the bitch hit the floor and couldn't get back up. Her girls were coming, from left to right, and I was laying them hoes out with my tray. I felt someone back-to-back with me, and when I looked over my shoulder, it was a girl named Kia helping me whup their asses. We fucked those hoes up!

When the lunch staff broke the fight up, there were three bitches knocked unconscious from my tray still on the floor. I was filled with rage when they dragged me to the principal's office along with Kia and the others. I was still hyped up; I wanted war. When they got me calmed down, they asked my side of the story and I told them. She asked me why I'd used my tray as a weapon. I told her because it was in my hand. Then I told her I hoped they were all dead. She sent me straight to the social worker with a note that said, "Check her mental state."

We all ended up kicked out of school for three days. When it was time for me to get reinstated, they tried to stop me from coming back to that school. They said I needed mental help. Mrs. Morgan went off. She told the principal I would be back the next day, and if she gave me a problem, she would show her I wasn't the only one who needed mental help! We walked out.

The next day I was back just like Mrs. Morgan said. I swear she had my back. I saw Kia and thanked her for also having my back. We became close after that. Kia was my one and only friend. High school was a breeze for me after that. Everybody respected me and knew better than to step in my way. Kia and I ran the school.

Twelfth grade year finally came; I was still running shit and I was head of the cheer team. Nikki never came back to the school after the beat down I gave her. All of her so-called fiends were now my flunkies.

Six months before graduation, I got the worst news of my life. Mrs. Morgan had been battling sickle cell and lost her fight. When I came home from school, the police and the body truck were outside. She'd passed away in the living room on the floor. I passed out; the only person I had who loved me like I was her own was gone. I figured God had to hate me. I had just turned eighteen, so I was on my own. Mrs. Morgan left me everything—the house, the car, and eighty thousand dollars. I knew it would only last me for a while, so I had to find a job. Kia had a friend who danced at the Pretty Kitten; she hooked us up and got us in. This was the beginning of my life as a stone-cold killer.

Chapter 1 ✳ *Family Ties*

Three years have passed. I'm twenty-one and the baddest bitch in the bar. My ass is fat, my breasts are perfect, and I am beautiful. I don't have to fuck to get money. All I do is dance. I make at least a thousand dollars a night, and I only work Thursday, Friday, and Saturday. Three thousand a week is good for me. Plus, I didn't blow the money Mrs. Morgan left me. I have it all—a nice, big house, a nice car, and money in the bank.

My house has four bedrooms, so I let Kia move in. I hate being alone in that house. Not only had I killed Mr. Morgan in that house, Mrs. Morgan had died there as well. I'm not going to move though; it's paid for and all mine. I love my life. I feel like it's me against the world and I'm winning. I keep up with my birth mom through letters and I keep money on her books as well. I try to make it my business to fly out to visit her every three months. I told my mom everything; I knew she wouldn't judge me. She doesn't like the fact that I strip, but she's proud that I'm keeping my head above water.

Kia and I start the search for my brothers and sister, who'd abandoned us years ago. It is strange to me how they'd left and never looked back. I'd promised my mom I would never stop searching for them. When I finally find my sister, I didn't like the bitch I found. She is a stuck-up bitch, married to a rich, white doctor, and they live in Rochester Hills, Michigan. She drives a 745, and although she has her masters in criminal justice, she's never worked a day in her life.

I am kind of angry at the fact she is doing so well now. She has no excuse why she's never come to find her little sister. We meet for lunch at a restaurant in downtown Detroit; I guess the bitch doesn't want me at her house. I am a little late getting there, but when I walk in, I know exactly who she is. She is pretty as hell, hair down her back, dressed up in a pants suit with her Gucci shoes and bag. I smile looking in the window at her. She looks like an older me, but a younger version of my mom, perfectly put together. I can tell she is irritated because I am late. I walk in and stand in front of her.

"Reagan, is that you?" she asks.

"Yes, Aleeah, it's me," I reply.

"Oh my God, you're beautiful," she says as she hugs me tightly.

"And so are you."

She pokes me in one of my boobs, asking, "Are those real?"

I laugh. "Yes, they're real. Nothing on this body is fake."

I assume she thinks they're fake because they are so much larger than hers. We are shaped alike, but our breasts are very different in shape and size. *'Hater,'* I think.

We sit down and order our food. I am staring and smiling, I can't believe it is really her.

"So how have you been, Reagan?"

"Good, lately. I had a rough start at life, but I'm finally happy now."

"That's good."

I can see her checking me out. She looks at my Louis Vuitton bag on the seat, staring so hard I can tell she is checking to see if it is authentic. I break her stare.

"So tell me about yourself."

"Well, I am married, no children and no job. My husband's a doctor. I have two dogs, a big house, and, oh yeah, my husband is white. That just about sums it up," she says with a big smile on her face.

I already know most of this stuff because I'd investigated before our meeting. "That's nice. So now that the ice is broken, I need to ask you some questions. Like why did you run away? Well, I kind of know the answer, but why didn't you ever come back?"

The look on her face shows she is uncomfortable and gets real quiet.

"Where were you when dad died? Did you even care to see what happened? Did you know mom went to prison for his murder? I mean, you had to know I was left in foster care. Why in the hell didn't you look for me?"

With tears in her eyes, she looks out the window. "I was happy when they told me Jaycion was dead. I hated him!" She pauses. "I knew seeing you wasn't a good idea," she says, looking me dead in the eyes.

"WHAT? ARE YOU FUCKIN SERIOUS? IF YOU DON'T WANT TO ANSWER THE QUESTIONS, THEN DON'T! NO NEED TO BE NASTY TOWARDS ME," I yelled.

"There's a lot you don't know, little girl. I choose not to relive my past; hell, I don't want to visit it either. I'm here now, and that's all that matters."

"That's all the matters to you. I, on the other hand, want to know why my only sister never looked for me. I needed you."

"You didn't need me, you had your mom. I was her first daughter, but you were her favorite. I knew she would protect you."

"Bitch, you mean to tell me my life was a living hell because I was the favorite? I killed Daddy protecting her. She's in prison doing *my time*. My childhood was fucked up, and you got the nerve to be M.I.A. because of jealousy? Do you know my story? All the shit I've been through? You could have come and got me, but instead, you marry yo' white man, sit on yo' high horse, and say fuck where you came from! What about Momma?"

She cuts me off. "You aren't *my* child, so I wasn't responsible for you, and as far as Momma, fuck Momma. She didn't protect me; she didn't give a fuck about me. I don't care what happens to the bitch."

It is so obvious she doesn't know me. I stand up, face soaked from my tears, and I slap the dog shit out of her ass. Then I take my glass of red wine and throw it in her face. "Now add this moment to your fucked-up past. Go back to yo' white man and act like you don't remember your mother and father, your only sister, and your brothers. Bitch, you're Jaycion's daughter no matter who saved you."

I grab my purse and leave out the restaurant. She isn't far behind. She watches as I jump in my Range Rover. I ride past her getting in her 745.

"Yeah, bitch, I got money, too. The difference is I made mine!"

I smash out with rage in my heart. I cry all the way home. If she wasn't my sister, I would have stabbed her for talking down on our mom.

After that meeting, I start not to look for my brothers, but since I'd promised my mom I would, I continue my search. My brothers are so much older than me that I barely remember them. I have some old pictures of when they were young, but that's all. I put my girl Kia up on the situation with my sister. She tells me, blood or not, she is my sister 'til the end. I have her back and she's always had mine, even when we didn't know it.

We get on the computer and start looking for my three brothers, Mario, Maurice, and Marquest Jimerson We find Mario and Maurice within minutes. Mario is serving time in prison for having a sexual relationship with an underage girl. He has been locked up five years already, and he only has two more to go. Maurice is locked up for robbery; he has one year left. He's served fourteen and he's been locked up since before Dad died.

I can't find Marquest. Seeing how everyone else is fucked up, I just know he has to be dead or something. He is the youngest boy, one year older than Aleeah, so he should be thirty-two. I am exhausted from my long day, plus I am flying out to see Mom in the morning. I jump in the shower and hit the sheets. This time Kia is flying out with me.

We get up early and go to the airport. Visiting my mom always means so much to me. I never miss a visit. I owe her that much.

When we get there, I have to tell Mom all about my meeting with my sister. She says she doesn't know why my sister hates her. She also tells me to keep trying to be involved with her. Her final request is to have Aleeah come visit her so they can talk things out. She really wants to know why she's so bitter. She also asks me to keep searching for Marquest, and to start writing Mario and Maurice. I agree; anything she asks of me, I'll see that it's done. I can never repay her for what she's doing for me. Our visit is nice. We say our goodbyes and off we go.

Chapter 2 ✳ Night Life

Tonight the club is going to be hype. It's my girl Kia's birthday party. Kia's stage name is Thunder and mine is Storm. When we dance as a team, they play some ol' rainy-ass, water-dripping, hype music, and introduce us as, "The best thunderstorm ever!" We are the dream team, and the hoes hate us. A lot of bitches know us from school, and know we can and will beat a bitch down, so they keep their distance.

When we get to the club, it is off the chain. The lot is full, no free spaces except for the ones reserved for us dancers. Cars are double-parked and the line is wrapped around the building. We park and jump out. The niggas in the crowd start yelling out our names. We are so flattered, but we continue to walk into the building. Feeling like stars, we mob through the bar, throwing our hands up, speaking to all the people we know.

We go to the dressing room to get dressed for our set. Kia's birthday outfit is cold. It is pink and white, her favorite colors. Her boots are knee-high, pink, and studded. Her thong and bra are hand-knitted and fit perfectly. She walks out to *Cold Blooded*. When she hits the stage, the niggas go nuts. Hell, a few bitches are front and center as well. Thunder rips that stage apart. Money is everywhere. Smiles, the stage keeper, gathers all her money before we start our set together.

The DJ hypes the crowd up before I make my grand entrance. "Hey, y'all already had the Thunder, now y'all gotta have the Storm. Put yo' glasses in the air and yell, 'Let it rain'," the DJ says on the mic. The bar goes wild; people are looking around to see which way I'm coming. I surprise everyone when I fall from the roof of the bar. The music is loud with storm sounds, but once my feet touches the stage, *She's a Bad Mama Jama* comes on. My outfit matches Thunder's, with just a few different details. My boots are all white and they come up to my thighs.

We work each side of the stage. The DJ puts on some twerking music and we bounce our asses to the same beat as we dance to the music. Money is falling out the air. Niggas are throwing hundred-dollar bills. I look into the crowd and notice our regulars, but there's a group of niggas throwing nothing but hundreds. I use my eyes to keep them mesmerized. I watch them as they watch us work the stage.

There is one particular guy who stands out to me. He is fine as hell. He has his Gucci hat pulled down low, but I can still see his face from the side. He doesn't look me in my eyes, but he continues to throw money at me.

"Stuck-up nigga," I say to myself. Being the pretty bitch I am, I walk away and go to the other side of the stage. When our set is over, Smiley hands us bags of money. We go backstage and count our dough. We make enough to split evenly, but it's Kia's birthday, so I give her half of mine as a gift. This bitch has been my ride-or-die for a long time and I love her like no other. We put our money in lock up and change our outfits for lap dancing.

We walk through the bar as niggas pull and tug at our arms. This one nigga has the nerve to cuff me on my ass. I give him the cute, "Don't you do that" face, and keep it moving. I do a couple of dances for my favorites, but I'm really checking for dude in the Gucci hat. I know I've never seen him before, but that nigga was throwing mad paper. I work the floor until I've hit every corner, and when I don't find him, I go into the dressing room.

The girls in the back are carrying on about a guy named Face and his boy Stone. "That nigga Face is looking good girl. Where's he been? I haven't seen him in a while," Candy says.

"Girl, I heard he left town after they shot him up. Shit, he was fucked up. They hit his ass with an AK and a gauge. It's a miracle he made it," Diamond says.

"Girl, he left town so he could get better. Now he's back on a mission. Did y'all see how deep they were?" Cashmere asks.

I am just listening. Whoever this nigga is, he use to be the man and maybe he still is. I continue to listen and suck up info on the two men everybody was so happy to see. They have to be the only two in the front I didn't recognize. Kia comes and cleans herself off.

"I am ready to go," she says, irritated as hell.

"Let's go then."

"I can't leave yet. I have people here just because it's my birthday. I'll just get dressed, go out there, and talk to a few people."

"Cool," I say.

We both get dressed and do just that. We end up staying 'til the bar closes. We never, ever do that. We leave out the side door, closer to where my truck is parked. On our way out, that same guy from earlier who cuffed my ass, does it again.

"Look, nigga, when I have my clothes on, I'm off duty. Don't put your fuckin' hands on me. I ain't naked and yo' broke ass ain't thrown no money all night," I say as I try to get pass.

"Bitch, please! I wish I would pay you to touch yo' ass. Bitch, you work in a strip club; that ass is up for grabs," he says.

Kia jumps in front of me, knowing things are about to get real ugly. "Hey, why don't you just get the fuck on, nigga! Ain't nobody got time for you or yo' bullshit!"

We turn around and walk out the door. This muthafucka follows us. I know he's on some bullshit, so I pull my pocket knife out my back pocket and hold it in my hand. As soon as we approach the parking lot, he says, "Give me those bags since you hoes wanna act stupid!"

I turn around ready to stab his ass and notice he has gun. My heart drops in my shoes. I have sixteen hundred dollars in my bag. I gave Kia one thousand to add to the two thousand she'd made. There ain't no telling what else she has. Pissed off, I begin to take off my backpack, mad as hell we tried to be slick and used the side door. Just as I'm handing over my bag, the dude with the Gucci hat walks up and lets two shots loose, hitting our robber in the chest.

"I hate it when hoe-ass niggas pick on sweet, little ladies," he says as he walks up and shoots him dead in the head.

We're shocked. Kia is really shaken up. She has never seen anything like this before. I play it like I'm shocked, but it's really nothing new to me. The way I was feeling about ol' boy, I'm glad he's dead.

"Y'all get on outta here. I'll clean up this mess," Gucci hat says.

We take off. We jump in my truck and leave. I don't want anybody asking me shit. Kia is still in a daze.

"You okay, boo?" I ask.

"Not really. That was crazy. Ol' boy let my man have it."

"Girl, thank God he came. Dude probably was going to kill us. We know his face too well. Trust he wasn't going to let us just walk away."

"You're probably right. Shit, I need a drink!"

We make us some drinks when we get to the crib. As we discuss the night's events, I begin to have flashbacks of the night I shot my father. Tears start to fall from my eyes, I can't control them. I've never told Kia the truth about my childhood. I wanted her to see me as a normal person.

"What's wrong, Reagan?" Kia asks.

"I have to tell you something. You have to promise me you'll love me the same," I say to my ace-boon-coon.

"Girl, I love you and all your flaws; nothing will ever change that."

"I wasn't creeped-out by that nigga being murdered because I've killed before." I pause to take a look at her face. She has a look on her face that reads she can't believe it.

"How? When? I've known you since we were kids."

"That's just it: I was a kid and I was protected. My mom didn't kill my father; I did. I know you think I'm a virgin, but I'm not. Mr. Morgan, my adopted father, raped me when I was twelve. I killed him, too. Mrs. Morgan took the rap for me as well. This is why I hate men. You always ask me why I don't date. I don't trust men and I don't like them. I started dancing, and the money was so good, I had to tolerate them." I pause to clean my face.

"Girl, I thought you were a lesbian. I was just waiting on you to tell me you wanted me," Kia says.

We look at each other and burst into laughter. "That's why I love you, Kia. You bring out the best in me."

"I love you, too, girl. Your secret is safe with me. Hell, I'm sure they deserved just what they got," Kia says. She puts her arms around me and whispers, "I always knew you were crazy."

I push her off me. "Fuck you and goodnight."

I sleep well; knowing my girl still loves me makes all the difference in the world to me. We wake up the next morning wondering if we should go to work. We decide to go because not showing up would make us look some type of way.

We go to the bar and I dance my stage set but decide not to work the crowd. Kia does both. I am focused—listening, watching, and waiting to hear someone talk about what happened last night. I'm standing at the bar ordering my drink when this dude comes and stands next to me. First, I notice he smells so good. I look down at the LV shoes, then I stroll up to his midsection. Yup, he has the belt to match.

When my drink is ready, the bartender says fifteen-sixty. He says, "I got you." I take my hand out my purse and look up. This nigga's face is fucked up; it kind of scares me.

"Thank you," I say.

"You remember me?" he asks.

"No, I don't."

"Baby girl, I ain't gon hurt you. It was only yesterday I laid a nigga down for you." He pauses. "You remember me now?" he says as he turns and looks me dead in my eyes.

I'll be damn! I can't believe my eyes. It is him—the pretty boy who wore the Gucci hat. I only saw him from his good side. The left side of his face is fucked-up. He has to be the nigga they call Face.

"Okay, I remember you now. I didn't see this side of you. I wasn't being funny. I apologize," I say as I reach up and touch his face.

He gently takes my hand off his face. "Why would you touch my face? That's pretty brave of you. You don't know if I'm contagious."

"Let me guess, you're Face," I say.

"Let me guess, the face gave me away." We laugh.

"Can we sit and talk?" he asks.

"Sure."

This nigga is fine as hell, even with his fucked-up side. His walk, his talk, and even his style are so fly. We walk over to the VIP booth where all of his boys are.

"Y'all know Storm, right?" he asks his crew.

Everybody gives me the "what's up" head tilt. We haven't sat down good and all the damn strippers in the bar are flocking around, begging to give him a dance.

"You good, Face?" this dancer named Ivy asks.

"Yeah, I am good, ma. I'm chilling with baby girl for the night," Face says.

Ivy gives me a dirty look as she walks away. "DON'T GET MAD 'CAUSE YA NIGGA CHOSE ME!" I yell. Everybody bursts out laughing.

"I like that feisty shit, little mama. You didn't see me watching you last night?" Face asks.

"Nope," I lie.

"You're a cold piece of work, little mama. I was really digging your moves," Face says.

I smile, call over my favorite waitress, and order a bottle of Moet. I have to show this nigga I'm not a money-hungry stripper. I'm not at all impressed with his money. When Cam sets the bottle on the table, Face starts going in his pockets. I wave my hand and tell him it's on me. He just smiles.

"Damn, baby, I swear you're my kind of lady."

"So tell me about yourself, Mr. Face."

"Well, my name is Semaj, which I think is a really cool name. Well, you see my face. It's self-explanatory. I was fucking this little chick on the eastside, and she had a man, but didn't tell me. I took his bitch and it left a bitter taste in his mouth. His name was

Marko and he was supposed to be the man on his side of town. He was acting like a bitch; he called my phone and told me to leave his bitch alone. We had words and I thought that was it. I kept smashing his girl and that nigga sent his goons for me.

"I kind of think she set me up. The night they hit me, I was supposed to meet her. I usually kept my niggas posted, but I was on an ass mission. My mom always told me a hoe will get you killed. Them niggas fucked me up and left me for dead. The nigga who shot me in my face was an ol' hating-ass nigga. After he shot me, I heard him say, 'Pretty motherfucker, they gon have to keep your casket closed.'

"I was still breathing. I laid there, still as hell, thinking, *They'd better not let me live.'* They went in my pockets, and took my money and my glasses; they even took my Rolex. They burned out the parking lot and left me right by my truck. When they ambushed me, I was getting out my truck, so the door was opened. I pulled myself up and grabbed my phone. I called the police then my mom. I blacked out after that.

"I woke up two months later in the hospital. My mom flew me to her sister's house in Florida so I could heal. It's been a year now and I'm back with a purpose."

I gave him a funny look. "Damn, that's deep!" I say.

"Yeah, I'm deep, baby. So tell me about you."

I tell him what I want him to know. Hell, I ain't friendly with my info. Shit, I ain't even tell his ass my real name. He's cool and all, but he is still a customer—a crazy one at that. I'm willing to get to know him, so we kick it a little longer. Kia gets dressed and joins us in the booth for drinks. We're having a good time, and

Face's boy Stone is all over Kia. They introduce themselves and begin to talk.

"Damn, baby girl, you look so familiar," Stone says to me.

"I was just thinking the same thing. Not sure where I know you from, but I'll figure it out," I say.

"Shit, it's got to be from here. I be in this bitch a lot," Stone says.

"Yeah, it might be."

We sit and talk to them until the bar closes. This time they walk us to our car. I whisper in Face's ear, "What did y'all do with ol' boy's body? Nobody seems to know shit."

"What you talking about, baby girl? We ain't messy; we clean up our trash," Face says.

"Okay, cool; I've taken out the trash before, so I know what you mean," I say, smiling.

Kia and Stone are exchanging numbers. Face and I do the same. Face's boys are standing around on guard. They protect that nigga like he's their king. We say goodbye and leave. They watch us pull out the lot then they pull out.

This is the beginning of a crazy kind of love.

Chapter 3 ✳ The Bond

Face and I have been dating for a year now. Kia and Stone kick it, but not on a regular. Stone has a woman in Ohio, so he is in and out. When he's here, Kia is his main chick. I still keep trying to remember where I know him from. The more he comes around, the more it seems like I knew him before. He's cool as hell though, so it really doesn't matter.

Face and I are like two peas in a pod. I really respect this man. He shows me nothing but love. We kiss, we touch, we even play around about sex, but when I tell him I'm not ready, he respects that. That alone makes me love him. I figure I'll tell him the truth about my situation when the time is right. Hell, I'd seen him murder a nigga, so we really should be on some trust shit. I'm just not comfortable telling people I lost my virginity to a rapist. I haven't been touched by a man since. I've never made love; I've always had a hateful feeling for men in my heart. I've always felt like they use their strength power and money to mistreat women.

Face is the first man I've allowed near my heart, and I think I love him. We really never talk about relationships, so we never use a title when it comes to what we share. We are just really close friends. We do everything together—shop, eat, drink, we even sleep in the same bed. Face has his own apartment, but he always stays at my house. We give parties and all kinds of gathering, and my house stays banging. Face is my right-hand man. We do everything together, like I said before.

Face doesn't have any children, but he has plenty of hoes, and they don't want to let his ass go. They hate me, but Face makes them hoes respect me, and I don't have to say shit. When they see us out, they speak and keep it moving. One day, we're at the mall and one of his rats comes up to him on some stupid shit. Face tells that hoe, "When you see me with my lady, you don't fuckin' approach me." She tries to show her ass in front of her girls, and he chokes her ass up. He tells her to never let that happen again or else. As we walk off, she gives me the look of death. I just smile. Face isn't for any bullshit, and that is that.

He keeps a .45 on his hip at all times. He buys me a pretty little .380. It fits perfectly on my small waist. We go to the range once a week to practice shooting. I am the shit; hitting my target isn't a problem for me. I'm ready for any issues that might arise. We're better than Bonnie and Clyde. Face has become my ride-or-die.

I finally break down and tell Face about my past. He is so mad he says, "If Mr. Morgan was still alive, I would kill him myself." He also says I am still a virgin because I didn't give my virginity away, it was taken. We always talk for hours, sharing our deepest secrets; he is my keeper.

I decide to let him go with me to meet my mom. She puts him on her visiting list, and we make our first trip together. He falls in love with my mom. He has mad respect for her because of what she did to keep me free. They talk like they've known each other for years. I can barely get a word in. It's cool; I am happy to have her approval. Face is my world and I have plans for us. We say our goodbyes and leave.

We fall asleep on the plane. We have a big party to attend later on tonight. When we get to the house, Stone is there with Kia. We walk in on their nasty asses fucking on the floor.

"Damn, hoe, you got a room, don't you?" I say playfully.

"BITCH, SHIT JUST KIND OF HAPPENED," Kia yells, trying to cover up.

"Girl, I done seen that ass a million times, so don't waste your time trying to cover it up," Face says as he walks past.

We all burst out laughing as I sit the picture we'd taken at the prison on the fireplace.

"Carry on, children, carry on. You'd better let him get that nutt or he'll get blue balls," Face says as we shut the door to my room.

For the first time ever, I want to fuck. Seeing them being intimate really turns me on. I've never had a good picture of what sex really should look like. The only picture I had was an ugly one of Mr. Morgan forcing him inside of me. What I just saw looked nice. The way Stone was touching Kia's body makes me feel some type of way.

Face is in the shower and I am geeking myself up to make a move on him. My mind is all over the place. Should I take a shower first, or should I just be naked when he comes out the bathroom? I decide to take a shower after him. Face comes into my room with water beads dripping off his broad shoulders. His back is looking wide and strong. He has his towel wrapped around his waist and I can see the print of his dick. It doesn't look hard, but it does look big. I can feel my pussy getting wet as I look him up and down.

I jump up, grab my T-shirt and panties, and head to the bathroom. I am hot and horny. I turn on the shower, take my clothes off, and find out the wetness I am feeling is blood. My Auntie Bloody Mary decides to stop by at the wrong time. I am pissed. What I thought was sexual juice is a bloody mess. I jump in the shower, clean myself off, get dressed in my house clothes, and take my ass a nap. When I wake up, everybody is getting dressed for the party.

"Hey, Sleeping Beauty, we thought you were never going to wake up," Face says.

"Well, I'm up; let me go wash this sleep off my body then I'll be ready," I say.

I get my clothes together and go freshen up. When I finally finish, everyone is ready. We jump in Stone's truck and roll out. We get to the club and it is off the chain. Niggas and bitches are everywhere. The rest of Face's crew meet us at the party. He doesn't really travel to big events without his whole crew.

We don't stand in the line. Face is a VIP at every club he messes with. They treat him like royalty. We have a nice booth in the back of the club. Of course Face orders bottles of Patron and 1738. The waitress has everything set up for us. We walk to our booths while everybody watches. Groupies are checking out Face and his boys. Kia and I are the only women with eleven men, so you know we stand out. Bitches are looking so hard I have to put the mean-mug on. The music is banging, the vibe nice. This party is a big blast.

Kia and I hit the dance floor and we're throwing down. A crowd of niggas stand by and watch. Bitches watch as well, some are hating and others are pumping us up. I notice one guy trying his best to make eye contact with me. I avoid him purposely. Not sure about my relationship with Face, I don't want to be disrespectful. We don't have a title, but he keeps his hoes in check, so I have to follow suit.

I tell Kia I'm leaving the dance floor. Once I get back to our area, Face is standing up, looking at the dance floor hard as hell.

"Damn, Face, what's out there that has your attention? You're looking mighty hard," I say.

"Ol' boy in that blue jacket was checking you out, wasn't he?" Face asks.

"Yeah, and I walked away," I answer.

"Baby, I need you to distract his hoe-ass. That nigga was with them when they ambushed me."

I give Face a crazy look. "Okay, so what you want me to do?" I ask.

"Go dance with that nigga," Face says.

My favorite Sierra song comes on, so I hit the dance floor once more. I am dancing so sexy that nigga is damn-near in a trance. I look him in his eyes as I would do a paying customer at the bar. He gets closer and closer to me, until he is close enough to touch me. This nasty motherfucker has the nerve to ask me how much I would charge to go home with him.

"I'm not for sale," I say as sexy as possible, when I really want to go-the-fuck-off. I look up at Face and he's saying to get his number. I turn up my lip to let him know I'm pissed, but I go ahead and keep kicking it with dude. "Look, maybe we need to start over, right? Give me your number and maybe we can meet up for drinks," I say as I continue to dance, grinding on him.

"Here's my business card. It has my cell and my shop number on it. Now don't get it twisted, baby girl. You fine-as-fuck, but I'm not looking for a relationship. It's all fun for me. I'm just looking for a good time; you know, good company, a little shopping spree, and some good pussy. With that being said, I'm up front about what I want. If you're not interested, don't call."

I just nod my head as I throw up the okay sign. This nigga is a trip and I would have cussed his ass out any other day. Since Face has me fucking with this silly-ass nigga, he gets a pass. I dance my way off the floor thinking he'd just made my asshole pucker. I go to the restroom to freshen up, pissed I had to play like I was interested in that fool.

When I come out the restroom, there's a big commotion in the corner by our booth. All I can think about is Kia. I push my way through the crowd. Once I get there, I see Face and his boys fighting with ol' boy I was just dancing with. Kia has a bottle, going nuts on them niggas. My bitch doesn't play; if some shit jumps off and you're with her, she is going to bang. I grab my blade from under my left breast and start sticking niggas. Blood is flying everywhere. Niggas don't know who or what hit their asses. That nigga I was on the floor with is going head-up with Face. I sneak under the crowd and stick him in his side three times. I grab Face's arm and pull him out the crowd.

Kia yells, "LET'S GO."

We all scatter toward the door. We jump in our rides and smash out. Kia has blood everywhere.

"You okay, Kia?" I ask my girl.

"Yeah, I'm good. Shit, some nigga hit me in my mouth and busted my lip!"

"Y'all ain't no joke. Y'all are some real chicks, had our backs in that muthafucka!" Stone says.

"You thought you were fucking with some hoes?" I ask. We all laugh.

"Shit, I pushed Kia out the way, trying to protect her; next thing I know, she jumps over my shoulder with a Mo bottle. That shit was crazy. Where-the-fuck you pull that blade from, Storm?" Stone ask.

"Shit, I keep me a blade in my bra. I am cold with it, too. Them niggas don't know who stuck 'em," I say as we all laugh.

"What we gon do with y'alls crazy asses? I ain't never had a chick have my back like that. That shit was all love for real," Face says.

I just smile. He really doesn't have a clue how much I love him. We all pass out when we get back to the crib. We are sore and tired from the fight. Damn! It was a crazy night. Before I fall asleep, I watch as Face drifts off to La-La land. He looks so worried. It's like he's fighting a battle he just can't win. I kiss him softly on his lips and he opens his eyes.

"I love you," he whispers.

"Ditto," I whisper back.

This bond is now complete. I fall asleep in the arms of the man I've allowed to have my heart.

Chapter 4 ✷ The Haunting Truth

One Week Later . . .

I woke up in a cold sweat last night. I kept having horrible dreams. My dad and Mr. Morgan were chasing me. It was like I just couldn't get away. I would always wake up when they caught me. I don't know what this dream means, if anything at all. It's a recurring dream I've been having since I was a child. The only difference is, when I was young, they never caught me. I really want to know what this dream means. I was shaking so bad Face woke up.

"Baby, what's wrong?" Face asked.

"Bad dream, baby. That's all. Go back to sleep; I'll be ok."

Face put his arms around me and held me until I drifted off to sleep. He was my knight in shining armor.

I wake up to breakfast in bed. Face has cooked grits and eggs. He fixed toast and made me a bowl of mixed fruit, with a big glass of orange juice. I've never had a boyfriend, so I'm thinking, *'If this is what it's like, I'm all in.'* We sit in bed and eat breakfast together. We talk and laugh. I talk about my family and how we ended up out of touch with one another. I share tears talking about my past; it hurts so badly, all the things I've been through.

Face tells me a lot about himself I didn't know. His father was killed by his mom's brother. His dad raped his mother and she got pregnant; when she told her brothers who raped her, they'd gone out looking for him, and when they found him, they beat him to death. She didn't find out she was pregnant until she was three months and she decided to keep him. She said it wasn't his fault she was raped, and he deserved a chance to live. Face says he hates his dad for what he did to his mom, but he also wishes he could have met his family on his father side.

He has a bond with his mom and they are very close. I guess you can say he's a mama's boy. His mom got married, and after five years of being his mother's only child, she gave birth to his little brother Rodney, then his twin sisters, Shayla and Kayla. Face says he always felt left out when it came to father time. His siblings had their father, and he just couldn't get with the whole stepdad thing. That made him and his mom even closer.

When he turned fifteen, he started hustling. His stepdad was the provider and took care of his children, but he'd always denied Face. His mom hated her husband for that. At that time, she had no income of her own, so she felt she had to stay. She start stealing her husband's money to provide for Face. When he found out, he beat her really bad. When Face got home and saw his mom all beat up, he waited on his stepdad to get home and he beat him with a baseball bat. He was hospitalized but he survived. When he got out of the hospital, he took his kids and left.

Face promised his mom he would make a way. He hustled hard and stayed on top. Things were back to what Face called the good times—it was just him and his mom again. Face had always felt some kind of anger towards his siblings because they were treated so much better than he was by their father. It really didn't faze him they were gone. They would come to see their mom sometimes, but not on a regular basis. When their dad was mad at Face's mom, he would keep them away for long periods of time. Once they got old enough, they started to come over on their own, but by that time, Face was always out in the streets. He'd never formed a bond with his siblings. That's kind of my same situation. My siblings left me and never looked back.

Our conversation is interrupted by my cell phone ringing off the hook. I try to ignore it, but it is ringing nonstop. "Go ahead, baby, get your phone. It's got to be important the way it's ringing," Face says.

"Hello," I answer.

"Hey, Reagan, this is Aleeah. Please don't hang up. I know things didn't go well at our last visit. Please give me one last chance to explain. I really need to tell you the truth. You were so right. I can't just bury my past; I have to heal from it. Then maybe I'll be able to move on."

"Okay, where do you want me to meet you?"

"At my home. The address is 19607 Maple Hill Drive. Can you come today at one p.m.?"

"Yes, I'll be there."

We end our call and I fill Face in on our conversation. He says it's good she's had a change of heart.

"We'll see. I hope, for her sake, she acts right. If she doesn't, I'm whupping her ass," I say with my ugly grin on.

I lay back and put my arms behind my head, thinking about my life and all I've been through. I just can't understand why I've had to go through so much. Tears fill my eyes. I try my best to keep them from falling. I can't stop the waterfall that's running down my face.

"Baby, what's wrong?" Face asks.

"I just can't get over my past. I live in this bubble only because it allows me to pretend everything is okay. Face, I'm so scared of life and love. I mean, I want real love, unconditional love. Love that never dies," I cry.

Face holds my face in his hands and looks me in my eyes. "Look at me, baby. I'll love you 'til the end of time with all of my heart. I'll never leave you baby. I would die for you. You hear me? I would give my life to save yours. You have become my best friend, and if we never decide to become one, we'll always have this friendship."

I can't take in everything Face said fast enough. My heart melts. I kiss Face soft and slow, ready to give him all of me. He kisses me back as I caress his chest.

"Bae, you don't have to do anything you aren't ready to do. My love for you comes free. It's simply because of the person you are."

Face's eyes are glossy as he looks deep into mine. I climb on top of him, sitting on his pelvis bone. I begin to take off my shirt. Face sits up just a little and places my perfect breast in his mouth. The feeling that goes through my body is indescribable. I have never been touched like that before. The passion we share is real. For the first time in my life, I choose to give myself away.

Face moves slowly as he begins to pull off my panties. He picks me up and places me on my back. He pulls my panties off and begins to kiss my thighs. He works his way up until he reaches the special place I've held onto for damn-near a lifetime. I can't explain the chills that shoot through my body as his lips kiss my other lips for the very first time. My legs are shaking and my heart is beating at a runner's pace. The arch in my back keeps me lifted off the bed as he holds my legs over his shoulders and eats me like I am his last meal, leaving me soaked in juices from his mouth, which make the entrance to my love very accepting of his pleasure stick.

Grinding my teeth and gripping his back, I squirm as he enters into my love box. Trying to forget my very first time, I close my eyes tightly, thinking only of Face and how much I really love him. Tears cover my face as confusion takes over my mind, but love has finally taken over my heart. I embrace it and let it lead my body. I make love for the first time and it is with the man I truly love. I never imagined it could feel this good. My body is loose, enjoying pleasure and pain. I accept him into my world and I am hoping he'll stay forever.

"I love you, baby," Face moans in my ear.

"I love you, too," I say.

It is at that moment my body takes control. A feeling I've never felt before rushes through me and my pussy begins to throb. Face takes slow, long strokes as he feels my legs tighten around his waist.

"Let it go, baby. Let your juices flow all on daddy's dick," Face is whispering in my ear.

I can't control the high-pitched tone that escapes my lips as I yell out in ecstasy. *'This has got to be an orgasm,'* I think.

Face picks up the pace, and shortly after, he, too, yells out in ecstasy. We hold each other for what seems like forever. I am so into Face and what we've just done, I almost forget about the meeting with my sister.

"Face, I need to get up," I say as I pat him on his back.

"Baby, do you have to? I just want to lie inside you; you feel so good."

"Baby, I have to meet my sister."

"Oh, I forgot," Face says as he moves himself off me.

I am already late but I don't care; it is worth it to me. I call to tell her I'm running behind and I'll be there shortly. She's fine with that. I jump in the shower and wash my body. I put on some True jeans and a cute Try shirt, grab my Gucci belt, my Gucci shoes, and the biggest Gucci bag I have. I am still being petty; I have to let her know I have a couple of dollars, too. I kiss Face and dart out of the door. My mind is all over the place. I just can't stop thinking about Face.

I pull right up to Aleeah's house. I used my GPS, so it was easy to find. I park my truck in front of her house and get out. As I take that long walk to the door, my hair is blowing in the wind, my bag dangling from my arm, and I am looking like a million bucks, if I must say so myself. I am doing a last-minute check on my whole look, when I am greeted at the door by Aleeah.

"You look good, boo," Aleeah says.

She startles me. I hadn't expected her to be right there at the door. "Thanks," I say as I walk inside.

Her home is beautiful. It looks like some shit that would be on *Cribs*. This Gucci shit I have on means nothing at this point.

"Have a seat. Are you hungry?" Aleeah asks.

"No, thank you. I'm fine," I answer.

"Well, how about a glass of wine?" Aleeah offers.

"Yes, I'll take a glass of wine."

She comes out of the kitchen with two crystal glasses filled with a dark red wine.

"Show off," I say under my breath.

"Did you say something?" Aleeah asks.

"Oh no," I say, embarrassed that she heard me.

"Well, let me start by apologizing for our last visit. There is so much you don't know about what caused me to act the way I did. I'll start by saying I'm happy you found me. It's just, when I saw you face-to-face, it brought back all the bad memories about my life I'd never wanted to face again. You were too young to know, but when I left, it was for my own safety.

"Dad was responsible for picking me up from school each day. He was never late. He was the best dad in the world to me, until one day he picked me up and had to make a run. I was sitting in the car putting on my lip gloss and dancing to the music. Dad got out the car to talk to a man who was sitting in an all-black Benz with tinted windows. I'll never forget that day. When Dad got back in the car, he was so upset. Dad owed this guy big money and he wanted it ASAP. He pulled up to Dad's car and rolled down his window. I could see his face. He was very handsome, clean-cut, and well-put-together.

"Even though I was seventeen, I was still pretty naïve and child-like, and I was in my own world, so I paid their conversation no attention until I heard Dad say, 'She's my baby girl.' See, Mr. Bean had promised Dad's bill would be wiped clean, but only if he could be the first to have my young, virgin body. Dad said, 'No, I'll have your money by the end of the night.' But this man had his perverted mind on me, so he told Dad he didn't have until the end of the night. Dad looked at me and said, 'Baby, I need you to save my life. I want you to go with this nice man and do whatever he needs you to do.' I looked at Dad with tears in my eyes. 'Are you selling me so you'll be debt-free?' He looked at me and said, "He's going to kill all of us if I don't pay up now. He wants you. You can save our family.'

"Scared for you and Mom at home, I got out the car. There was a woman in the car with him. He told her to get out and get in the backseat. He told Dad he would call him in an hour or two, or whenever he was done with me. That filthy old man took me to a hotel, and he did any and everything he wanted to me. He even had his lady friend join in. My innocence was stolen from me, my virginity stripped away, or should I say, I paid the price for my family to live. I cried so hard, it looked like my eyes were filled with fire." Aleeah begins to cry.

My eyes begin to water as I watch her try to fight her tears. My glass is empty and she notices I have drank all my wine. She goes into the kitchen and grabs the bottle. She fills my glass then adds more wine to her half-full glass. She begins to talk again.

"After they were done with me, I felt like shit. My body hurt and my heart felt no love. I hated them and I hated Dad. I felt dirty and I knew I would never forgive him for what he'd allowed to happen to me. That no-good man fucked me in every hole on my body. I was bleeding from my pussy and my ass. I was seventeen, but my body was still built like a child's. That grown-ass man, with a dick the size of a horse, with no respect or compassion, fucked me for hours. I could barely walk when he was done. They didn't even let me shower afterwards. They threw me my clothes and told me to come out once I was dressed." She held her head down and dropped more tears.

I couldn't believe what I was hearing. I felt even better about killing my dad now more than ever. No wonder he'd never looked for her. He knew what he had done. He told my mom he'd caught her making out with some boy on the side of the school, so Mom assumed she'd run away because he'd disciplined her.

"I'm so sorry that happened to you. Why didn't you tell Mom," I ask.

"Let me finish. They dropped me off outside of a liquor store not far from the house. When we pulled up, I jumped out so fast I fell, hit my knee, and it started to bleed. I jumped up and got into the backseat of Dad's car. I didn't want to look at him. This muthafucka had the nerve to tell Dad if he ever needed anything else, he could always pay with me. He pulled off laughing. Then he yelled out his window, 'Fresh pussy is the best pussy.' I ducked down and covered my face. I cried all the way home and Dad never said a word.

"When we pulled in the driveway, he said, 'You just saved your family; you should be proud. Never speak of this to anyone or they'll pay with their life.' I just said okay. I had already planned to run away. Do you remember the last time you saw me? I came in your room late at night. I woke you up and told you I loved you.

I kissed you on your forehead and I knew I would never see you again."

I start crying. My heart hurts so badly for Aleeah.

"I hated you and Mom because I felt it was y'alls fault I'd had to give myself to a stranger. I thought if I erased y'all, I would never have to remember what happened. You and Mom were attached to my past, so I chose to give y'all up as well. I'm sorry. I love you, Reagan, and getting this off my chest has closed that chapter of my life. I can finally move on," Aleeah says as she cries to me.

I get out my seat, barely able to stand, drunk from the wine. I put my arms around my sister and we cry together. I had no idea her reason for leaving would be so deep. We cry for three hours. I tell her my story and she also can't believe I've gone through so much. We bond at that very moment and become sisters again. She tells me she ended up marrying a white man because she hates black men because of how she was treated by them.

Her husband was one of her college professors when she met him, and when she graduated, they started dating. He'd put himself through school and became a doctor. They got married and they've been happy ever since they been together. I tell her about Face. I also tell her I am a stripper. She doesn't judge me; she says if she ever had to, she would do it, too. We are built for that type of shit.

I really enjoy my sister this time. We make a promise to stay in touch. I convince her to come with me to see our mother. It would be the best gift I could ever give my mom. She's been waiting on Aleeah to come back into her life. Mom has all her children names on her visiting list. She always believed one day they would come to visit her. We make arrangements to visit our mom that next week. After all is said and done, we depart with hugs and kisses.

"I love you, little sis," Aleeah says as I walk away.

"I love you, too," I say. I jump in my truck and exhale—one down, three to go. I am still on the hunt for Marquest. I won't stop looking until I find him dead or alive. I am going to find him.

Chapter 5 ✳ The Danger Zone

Things are going good between Face and I. We get together every day. I trust this man with my life, and I know he trusts me with his as well. Life has been treating me kind for the first time, so I have no complaints. We have lots of fun—partying and shopping—just doing it big, living it up. My sister has become an everyday-fixture in my life. Either she calls me or we visit.

I even got her to come to the bar to watch me dance. The look on her face was too funny. You could tell she'd never been in a topless bar before, but she said she had a ball. She was throwing money and taking shots; she even got out of her seat and danced a little bit. I enjoyed seeing her have so much fun.

Face has slowed up on coming to the bar. He said he becomes irritated watching other men touching my body. Most of the time, he's outside when the bar closes to make sure we are safe. For the past couple of months, the club has been jumping. Niggas from everywhere are in the building.

On the night of China Doll's birthday party, niggas are fooling. Eastside niggas come in the door starting shit with the westside niggas. The dancers are beefing over clients. Shit is crazy. In the midst of all the madness, I notice this dude staring at me. I play it off like I don't notice him. He sends one of his boys to ask me to come give him a private dance. I walk over to his booth and dude is fine. Shit, he smells like a bag of money he has so much of it in his hands—all hundreds!

"Hey, daddy, what can I do for you?" I ask.

"Baby girl, you know what I want."

"Well, I hope you wanna dance 'cause I don't do shit else," I say with an attitude.

"Money talks, shorty, and I've got five stacks that says you'll come home with me," he says, waving money in my face.

I laugh. "You can shove that shit right up your ass," I say as I turn to walk away. This nigga's got me fucked up. I stop in my tracks; he's grabbed my arm.

"Baby, look, I'm sorry. Let me start over. My name is Marko and I want to get to know you; you know, outside of here."

I give his ass the look of death. "Oh really? Well, you came all wrong, boo; you need a better game plan."

"You're right, sweetie; do you forgive me?" he asks.

"Yeah, but next time please use a different approach. Everybody doesn't fuck for money. My job is to dance and that's all I do," I snap.

"Okay, sweetie, here's my number and a stack just for your trouble. I apologize for the disrespect," he says and I walk away.

I be on my grown-woman shit. I don't have to sleep with these niggas to get what I want. I go to the dressing room to change. Kia is already there changing. When I'm ready to leave, we walk down into the showroom and people are scattering everywhere. Bitches are running up to me screaming that Face was in a shootout with the eastside boys. I can't get out fast enough. Kia and I dart to the front door once the gunshots stop.

My cell phone starts ringing. It is Face. "Bae, move fast! Get out and jump into your truck. It's safe now. The police are coming so I'll meet you at the corner."

"Okay," I say as I end the call.

We run out the bar to my truck like track stars. I meet up with Face at the gas station on the corner. I get behind him and follow him to the hood; surrounded by cars and big trucks, I feel safe. Face's boys make sure we're good. When we get to the hood, Face fills me in on what happened.

"Bae, them eastside niggas were in that bitch—the niggas who shot me up. When I saw them come out, I just started busting. I hit two of them, but I couldn't get that bitch-ass nigga, Marko. They surrounded him like he is God!"

"Marko?" I ask.

"Yeah, the nigga whose bitch I was fucking!" Face said.

"Baby, he just gave me his card and a thousand dollars. We got into it 'cause he was on some buying-pussy shit. When I checked his ass, he apologized then he gave me his card and the money," I say as I pass Face the card Marko had given me.

Face is very quiet, looking as if he is in deep thought.

"Let me get at him, Face," I say, ready to ride for my man.

"Bae, you can't get that nigga. He keeps his goons around. They say that nigga never travels alone," Face says.

"He wants some pussy. I can get him alone then off his ass," I say, pissed because he treated me like a hoe in the bar.

"I don't want you fucking wit' that nigga. I can't put you in harm's way."

"Trust me; let me put an end to this beef. I got you; I don't have to fuck him. I can kick it with him, find out how he moves, then I can let his ass have it," I explain.

"Hey, any nigga who offers five thousand dollars to fuck can be set up. He wants Storm badly," Kia says.

"Y'all might be right, but you got to be smart about this shit. One sign you're from the other side and they'll kill you," Stone says.

"Maybe you can meet him at a room and we can get them like that," Face says.

"I've got to get him alone in a place he trusts is safe," I say.

"She's right, Face. You saw how they surrounded that nigga. Trust they aren't gon let him go to no room by himself, not to get new pussy. She has to get close to him. He has to trust her. She's got to make him fall in love," Fatts says.

"If she's gon do it, she's gotta do it right. That's a hell of a role to play," Stone says.

"The thought of this nigga touching you makes me sick," Face says.

"This business, my nigga, is life or death; after tonight, shit gets really real," Fatts says, pacing back and forth.

I know I'm in too deep, but I also know Face would die for me. I am willing to do anything to help save his life. The power of the pussy is amazing. I know I'll be able to make this nigga fall me.

The fact that he's a handsome little fella is going to make my job easier. I've killed before, so I feel I can do this with no problems. The only difference is this time it will be a cold kill. I won't be the prey, I'll be the predator.

I love Face. He's saved my life once already. I can do this little job for him. As soon as things calm down, I'm on Marko's ass like flies on shit.

Chapter 6 ✳ The Mission

Three weeks have passed since we made our plans to make moves on Marko. I did a little research and found out why he's so hard touch. His father was Mark Anthony Clay, and although he's dead, he left his son a dope empire that came with loyal goons. He has OG's protecting him just because of his father's legacy. I got word he loves the eastside topless bars. They say he hits them on a regular. Ballers' Den is his favorite spot.

I've never danced on the eastside. Those hoes are too thirsty for me. I have to head east and *mistakenly* bump into Mr. Marko. I tell Kia my plan and she refuses to let me go alone, so we mob to the eastside. When we get there, there is no one in the bar. Shit, we be filling up by ten where I'm from. We go in and pay our payout. We order a bottle of 1738 and head to the dressing room. We open our bottle and sip while we got dolled up for the night.

Some dancers come in raving about these ballers who just came in the club; Kia and I just sit back and observe how everybody tries to be the first to hit the floor to get at these guys. I know one of the girls named Spice, so I ask her what all the fuss is about.

"Girl, Marko and his little brother King just came in, and these hoes act like birds when they come in. They got that bread. You know what I'm saying? I don't even fuck with them. I fuck with my regulars. Them niggas are so stuck up, they act like bitches," she says.

I give Kia that look, it's time to shine. The DJ introduces us: "Hey, y'all, we've got a treat for you tonight. Thunder and Storm will be gracing the stage in about five minutes, so get your money ready 'cause these bad chicks will be worth every dollar." Niggas start moving towards the stage. Although we don't come east much, niggas know us because they've been on the westside.

When we walk out, the place is now nicely filled. I scan the bar, looking for my target. "Bingo," I say out loud to Kia when I spot him.

"Now let's work," Kia says.

The crowd is going crazy as we prance across the stage. I watch as Marko and his crew throw money all over the place. I can see Marko looking at me, licking his lips. I am ready to make my move. I walk toward the end of the stage and make my ass clap. King comes over and puts five hundred dollar bills on my ass. Marko grabs him by his arms and whispers something in his ear. King steps back and Marko begins to throw money all over my body.

"What's up beautiful? You remember me?" he asks as I dance in front of him.

"Baby, I meet a thousand men a week, but none of them have left an impression like you did. Of course I remember you," I say, looking him in his eyes.

"Can I get a private dance, baby?"

"Sure; as soon as my set is over, I'll be right over."

I dance for the rest of the song that's on. When it's over, *Dance for You* by Beyoncé comes on. I walk over to Marko to begin his private dance. He's all in. I sing along with the song as I touch my body, slowly caressing my breasts. I place my legs across his lap so I can straddle his body. I look him in his eyes as I grind on his dick. Damn! He smells so good and his hazel eyes are putting me in a trance. This nigga is *fine!* I almost forget about my mission and his cocky-ass attitude.

I snap out of the spell his eyes have put me under and get back to work. I turn around so my dance will be easier. I bounce my ass up and down on his lap as he puts hundred-dollar bills in my thong. Occasionally, he rubs my ass or touches my breasts, tipping a hundred dollars. Hell, that's the least I can do.

"Damn, baby, your ass is so soft," he whispers in my ear.

He has a sexy voice and his hands feel so good rubbing on my body that I turn back around so I can face him. For some reason, I dance like I've never danced before. I grab Marko's head and hold it in the palm of my hands as I press his face between my breasts. I feel him lick the side of my neck and it sends chills through my body.

I dance for Marko the whole night. Keith Sweat's *Make it Last Forever* is the last song that plays. I have him mesmerized. I bounce on his dick until it's hard as a rock. He places small kisses on my neck. His lips are as soft and smooth as his hands.

"Damn, baby, you gon leave me like this? You see my man standing up for you?"

"That's my job. I didn't tell him to stand up. He'll be okay, sweetie." I kiss Marko's forehead. "Thanks for all the love, baby," I say as I begin to walk away.

"Hey, Storm, you need to call me, baby girl, please. I wanna get to know you outside this bar. Here's my card again, just in case you lost the first one," Marko says.

"I'll call you, boo, I promise." I wink and walk away. "Mission accomplished," I whisper.

When I walk in the dressing room, bitches are mad as hell. "Damn, Storm, you could have let someone else get a dance with Marko! You hogged all the money," Strawberry said.

"DON'T EVER COME ON ME LIKE THAT! IF HE'D WANTED YOU, HE WOULDN'T HAVE ASKED ME TO STAY. BITCH, IF HE'S THE ONLY NIGGA IN THE BAR WHO'S GOT MONEY, Y'ALL NEED TO STEP Y'ALLS GAME UP. GET SOME REAL NIGGAS IN THIS BITCH—OR REAL DANCERS—'CAUSE WHERE I'M FROM, WE BRING IN PLENTY OF NIGGAS WITH PAPER. WE DON'T FIGHT OVER ONE," I say, loud as hell.

"Bitches hate us everywhere we go," Kia says as we slap hands and laugh.

We clean up and head out the door. As we walk out, we see the groupies surrounding Marko and his boys. I did the "I don't see yo' ass" play-off and try to walk past. Marko sees me and pushes past his groupies.

"Hey, Storm, you and your girl wanna go grab something to eat?"

I look at Kia; she gives me the okay look, so I say cool. "Yes, we can go grab a bite to eat. Where y'all wanna meet up? I'm not leaving my truck here."

"Just follow me. Let's go to the casino," Marko replies.

I nod my head okay then call Face to fill him in on my night. He tells me to move slow and play that hard-to-get role. He says guys like Marko love it when beautiful women make him chase. I say okay and we end our call. We pull up to the casino and jump out.

Marko has a nice little entourage and they protect him like he is Michael Jackson. I begin to worry. Looks like I'm gon have to fuck or offer to fuck to get him alone. These niggas are like fuckin' solders when it comes to him. We go in, have a bite to eat, and it's really nice. He turns out to be a gentleman. We have so much fun, it feels funny. We laugh and tell jokes, then we go play the crap tables. We are having such a good time I hadn't noticed it is really late.

"I gotta go, Marko; it's late," I say.

"Okay, let me walk you to your car. I have a room here, so I'm good."

He gets a couple of his boys to walk with him. When we get to my truck, he opens my door and his boy Cleve opens Kia's door. Marko leans in and kisses me on my cheek.

"That was sweet." I say.

"I had a really nice time. I could get use to hanging without the banging," he says and laughs.

I give him a little smirk, shut my door, and pull off. "This is going to be harder than I thought," I say to Kia.

"Yup, it looks that way," Kia says.

Oh what a night.

Chapter 7 ✳ *Picking Up the Pieces*

Today starts off good. I've been a little tired lately, running from the east to the west on a regular. I've been working hard as hell trying to get Marko to trust me; he's a hard nut to crack. Surrounded by his boys at all times, it looks like sex is the only way I'll be able to get him alone. I'll have to think of a plan to off this nigga without his boys knowing I did it. Today isn't the day for that. I'm off duty for now. I have other things to do.

Aleeah and I are going to visit our brothers. We haven't seen them in years, and it is time we have a family reunion. It has taken so long for us to get on the visiting list, we are so excited we are finally cleared. Maurice is in Jackson, and Mario is in a little camp behind the Jackson facility, so it isn't going to be out of the way to see them both on the same day.

Aleeah picks me up and we hit the road. We stop, pick up some food, and eat on the road. We have the music blasting, and we are singing and dancing in our seats.

"Girl, I am so happy we're back together. I hate I missed out on you growing up," Aleeah says.

"Yeah, it probably would have been fun having you around," I respond. We are both quiet for a minute.

"Well, we're together now and I ain't going nowhere, so we got all the time in the world to catch up."

I look over at her and smile. We laugh and talk shit the rest of the way there. When we arrive, we decide to see Mario first. We don't have to wait very long to get to the back.

"VISITORS FOR MARIO JAMESON." The officer calls for us to be searched. After we are searched, we hold hands as we walk in to see our brother who has become a stranger. The officer directs us to his table, where he sits all alone, looking around. He looks past us. I guess they didn't tell him who is here to see him.

"Hi, Mario," Aleeah says.

"Hi," Mario says back.

Tears begin to fill my eyes as I look my brother in his. I can't believe I haven't seen him since I was a child and, yet, he looks so familiar to me. "I guess you don't know who we are."

"Of course I know who you are. How do you think you were able to get in? I only have three women on my visitors' list: Mom, Aleeah, and baby Reagan," he says as he stands up and opens his arms for us to come in for a hug. "Oh my God! I can't believe it's y'all. I've searched for y'all for so many years, then I just gave up."

"Do you know where Marquest is?" Aleeah asks.

"Yeah, he lives out of town. He use to visit before he moved, but now he just puts money on my books and that's it. He never sent me his new address or nothing," he answers.

"We want to find him as well. When we leave here, we're going to see Maurice. Then tomorrow we'll be going to see Mom," Aleeah says.

"How is Mom? And, Reagan, what really happened the night Dad died?" Mario asks.

I am quiet for a minute. Not knowing where to start, I tell Mario the truth. Every time I tell that story, my heart breaks—not for my father, for my mother. She's been sitting in prison all this time when it should have been me. I wipe tears from my eyes as my brother holds out his hand to grab mine.

"You did what the rest of us weren't brave enough to do. We were so afraid of him, we just ran and never looked back. I feel so bad for leaving you guys. I just lost it. I was out here like a crazy man and the guilt ate me up. I thought about y'all every day," Mario says through tears.

"It's okay; that's the past. We are here to start our future as a family. Just promise me when you get out, you'll come be with us," I say.

"No doubt, baby sis."

We laugh, we cry, we eat, and we catch up. We have a beautiful time with our brother. When our visit is over, we have one big group hug. We say our goodbyes and promise to return. We walk out the same way we came in, hand-in-hand.

"That went better than I thought," Aleeah comments.

"Yeah, it did go well. One down, two to go," I reply.

We make our way around to the other prison, walk in, and sign in. We take our seats. It doesn't go as smooth as it did with Mario. The guard comes out and tells us Maurice has denied his visit. We plead with her to explain to him we are his sisters and it is very important for us to see him. After waiting an hour, we are finally called to the back.

We know who Maurice is instantly. He looks just like Mario, but he's a little rough around the edges. His hair is braided to the back and the hair on his face is very thick. He is built like a rock. His arms look as big as my head. Unlike Mario, he doesn't look happy to see us. We walk in and his face is all tight.

"Hey, how are you?" I ask.

"I'm good; what's up with y'all?" he answers.

"Well, let me start by saying we're your sisters, and we're just trying to get our family back together," Aleeah says.

Before she can continue, he cuts her off. "For what? I ain't seen y'all muthafuckas in years. Far as I am concerned, I ain't got no family. What the fuck y'all really here for?"

Aleeah's mouth is wide open in disbelief.

"Look, nigga, ain't nobody gon kiss your ass! If you don't wanna fuck with us, we can leave," I say as I begin to stand up. I am sick of his ugly looks and his smart-ass mouth.

Aleeah pushes me back down into my chair. "Look, if we never come here again, that will be fine with me, but today, we're going to say what we came to say. Fuck your attitude! We all have a reason to be mad. Why don't you start by telling us yours!" Aleeah says.

He bursts out laughing. "We all got that one thing in common: Jaycion's fucked-up attitude and his smart-ass mouth."

We all burst into laughter. He calms down and begins to share his story with us. He tells us our father used to beat him and the other boys for any and everything. He also says he didn't run away; Dad told him to never come back. He says he was home alone with Mom and Dad when Dad started to beat Mama. He jumped in and hit Dad. After the fight was over, Dad said he had to leave because there was only one man of the house. He left and never look back."

He also wanted to know the truth about what happened to Dad. He said Mom was too weak to protect her children from the monster she chose to father us. He said he knew she didn't have the heart to kill Dad. Once again, I had to tell that story. Once everything is out in the open, the air thins out. We talk and reminisce about the parts of our lives together we do remember. The rest of the visit goes well. We make the same promise to Maurice as we did with Mario. We are rebuilding our family and this time we will keep it together.

We are tired and need to rest. We have a long day the next day; we are flying out to see Mom. I fall asleep on the ride home; when I wake up, we are in front of my house.

"Okay, girly, see you tomorrow," Leeah says.

"Okay, boo, be on time."

I go into the house and shower, then go straight to sleep. Sleep always feels better when you go to sleep happy. Morning comes and I am well-rested. I jump out of bed very excited. Today, my mom will get the one gift she's been waiting on for years. I haven't told her Leeah and I have been rebuilding our sisterhood. This day will be a total surprise to her.

I shower again and get dressed. I pull my hair straight back, do my makeup, and I am ready to hit the road. Before I can call Leeah, she is at the door. I am happy to see she is very excited to be seeing Mom once again.

"How do I look?" Aleeah asks me.

"Just like our mother," I respond. She smiles and we head out of the door. Our flight is beautiful; Aleeah is high class, so we fly first class. The food is excellent. We have so much fun. Every time we get together, we have fun and become a little closer. Remembering how my heart became cold is slowly fading away. When we finally arrive at the prison, Leeah is shaking like a wet puppy, nervous as hell.

"You okay?" I ask.

"Yeah, I just don't know what I should say or do; it's been so long since I've seen her. Oh well, I'll be fine; it's too late to turn back now."

"Stay right behind me so she doesn't see you right away. The look on her face will be priceless."

We check in and take our seats in the waiting room. Thirty minutes later, we are called to the back. The walk seems long and slow. My mom's face is glowing. She is beautiful; looking at her from afar is like I am looking at Aleeah. I look like my mom because I have some of her features, but Aleeah is her twin. As we get closer to Mom, I begin to cry. I am so happy I can bring her the only gift she's ever asked me for.

We are close enough to speak, but I don't say a word. I step aside and expose Aleeah's full body. At that very moment, I can see my mom's heart melt through her chest.

"Aleeah, baby, is it really you?" through tears and a big lump in her throat my mom asks.

Aleeah answers, "Yes, Mom, it's me."

My mom grabs Leeah and holds her so tight in her arms, all I can do is step aside and cry. I've finally done something good for the one who gave her life for me. I am bringing my family back together, or I will die trying. My thoughts are interrupted by my mom putting her hands on my face.

"Baby, you have made me the happiest woman in the world. How can I ever repay you? You have given me my life back. I don't know how you did it, but you did," my mom cries.

We have one big group hug filled with love, snot, and tears. We finally sit down. Words can't describe the emotions we feel at that very moment. After the tears are dried, Aleeah is able to tell Mom her truth. Mom sits there speechless. With her eyes wide open, she cries uncontrollable tears.

"I would have killed him then if you had told me that," Mom says.

"I was scared. I knew you feared him, so I didn't think you could protect me," Aleeah says.

"Look, we're here now and he isn't, so let's not let him control our future together. We can start from here; this is our new beginning," I say.

We tell Mom about our visit with the boys. She is happy we've finally gotten together. "Okay, so now you guys have to work hard to find Marquest," she says.

"We will," Leeah says.

Our visit with Mom goes great. You wouldn't even know she and Aleeah have been separated all those years their vibe is so good. We say our goodbyes and off we go. We talk on the plane the whole way home. When we get back to the airport, we jump in Leeah's car and head to my house.

"Well, what did you think of Mom?" I ask Leeah.

"She's beautiful inside and out. She seems like a different person. She's so happy and full of life. It's so sad I never saw her that way when she was with Dad, but in prison, she smiles like an angel."

"Well, she always tells me not to be sad she's in prison. She says I saved her from her slave master; that's what she calls him," I says.

When we finally get to my house, Stone is knocking at the door. "Who is that on your porch?" Aleeah asks.

"That's Kia's boyfriend."

"What's his name? From the side, he looks really familiar."

"His name is Stone. When I first met him, I told him the same thing."

"Oh well, I'll catch him another time. See ya soon."

I jump out the car and go straight into the house. I call Face; I am missing my man. He comes right over; we chill the rest of the day and talk about my mission. I tell him how Marko was all in and it's going to be really easy to get him alone. I don't tell him I think I'll have to fuck him to get him alone. Shit, as long as I get the job done, it really shouldn't matter. Tomorrow my mission continues.

Chapter 8 ✳ Nose Wide Open

Today, I awaken early. I receive a phone call from Marko requesting I meet him for breakfast. Getting right into character, I jump out of bed and get myself together. Having to leave the man I truly love sleeping in my bed, I realize I have a job that needs to be done, so I do what I have to do. I kiss Face on his forehead and leave.

I meet up with Marko at the House of Pancakes on 12 Mile and Evergreen. Now he is known to be an eastside nigga, but for some strange reason, we always meet in Southfield. I walk in and he is already seated. The waitress meets me at the door and escorts me to his table. I am shocked he is alone, or appears to be.

"Hey, beautiful," Marko says as he pulls my chair out for me to be seated.

"Hey, handsome, how are you this morning?" I respond.

"Much better now that you're here."

This man is so handsome, I can't help but blush when he speaks sweet words to me. I feel kind of bad about what is going to be his future. He seems like a really nice guy. Too bad he crossed my baby Face; he has to die. When I snap out of my thoughts, Marko is asking me a thousand questions about myself. He is really trying to get to know me.

"What do you want from me?" I ask him.

"Well, before I took the time to get to know you, I just wanted some pussy. Now I like being around you; I really enjoy your company."

"Wow, that's nice to know."

We order our food and continue our conversation. We are having a good time, laughing and talking. I can tell he is really feeling me. He's going to make my job easy because he is slowly falling for me.

"Let's go shopping," Marko says.

"Where you wanna go?"

"Somerset, that's my favorite mall."

"Well, let's go."

We finish our food, he pulls my chair out, and head out. I pay close attention to everything Marko does. He whispers in the waitress' ear as he hands her a hundred-dollar bill and we leave the building. While walking me to my car, Marko makes a phone call. Just like I thought, we are not alone. His boys are sitting in the parking lot all this time. He tells them his next move and they are ready to follow.

"Baby girl, leave your car here and ride with me."

I hesitate but still play my role. "Let me get my jacket," I say as I walk over to my car. I text Kia to tell her where my car is and where I'm headed. She shoots me back an okay.

I grab my jacket and jump in the car with Marko. He has the new Porsche, butterscotch inside and all white on the outside. His car is fly. "This nigga's getting major money," I say to myself.

We go to Somerset and spend five thousand dollars, most of it spent on me. Marko gets himself some Gucci boots, and a hat and belt to match. I get whatever I want. It's funny to me he wants to hold my hand as we walk through the mall. I am really uncomfortable, but know I have a mission to complete, so I have to stay in character. We have so much fun, it's hard for me to keep the connection business. I kind of enjoy Marko. He takes me back to my car and we part.

When I get home, Face is up, in the kitchen cooking. "Well, I see you have bags. What's going on?" Face says to me.

"Well, we went to breakfast, and after, he asks me to go to the mall with him."

"Did he pay for all that shit?"

"Yeah, he actually picked the stuff out himself. He says he wants to see me in it," I say as I put the bag on the table.

Face starts looking through the bags. "Damn, that nigga spent a grip!"

"Yeah, he's really feeling me. I'll be finished with this job sooner than I thought."

"Yeah, well, I'ma need you to hurry the fuck up. I'm sick of you hanging with that hoe-ass nigga. I know the game. He's trying to work on getting some of that pussy, spending all this money and shit. That nigga ain't me! Your ass had better remember your mission!" Face says angrily.

"Bae, I am on it. That nigga is good as dead! Yeah, he spent a little money. So what? You know that shit doesn't impress me. I know I'm working; everything I do with this snake is just a job. I'm going to get the job done, baby. This is all for you," I say as I walk away.

I go into my bedroom and shut the door. Face comes in shortly after as I am undressing. He walks up behind me and stands so close I can feel his dick resting on my ass. He moves my hair over to the front of my shoulder and begins to kiss on my neck. His kisses send chills down my spine. He moves down my back, kissing me all the way down to the crack of my ass. He slowly turns me around and kisses my pussy with so much passion my knees get weak.

Pushing my body against the wall and lifting my leg over his shoulder, he eats me like I am his favorite dish, causing my body to shake uncontrollably. I think I release so much fluid I begin to dehydrate. When he stands up, I can see his dick standing at full attention. He picks me up and places me on the bed. He sucks my breasts, one at a time, as he plays with my pussy with his finger. Once she is super-soaked, he places his dick deeply inside me.

This is only my second time making love, but I can feel the difference. It is wetter and feels so much better. It is skin-to-skin. I don't say what I'm thinking, but I don't understand why he didn't put on a condom. Hell, he is feeling so good inside me, I just go with the flow. Face is in his own world. It's almost like he's trying to prove something.

"Baby, is this my pussy?" he asks.

"Yes, baby," I whisper in his ear.

"This is my pussy? Is this my pussy? Tell daddy, baby. Tell me again, this is my pussy," Face requests.

"Daddy, this is your pussy. It's your pussy, daddy," I say in a high-pitched voice.

Face digs deeper and deeper inside me. He begins to call out in ecstasy. "This is your dick, baby. Take all of it. It belongs to you."

He goes faster and deeper until he reaches his moment of pleasure. He pulls his dick out and lets every drop of cum fall on my belly. Face lies down alongside me and places his head on my breasts. We lie there naked until we fall asleep. When I wake up, it is ten p.m., which means I am running late for work. Face is gone but he's left a note on my dresser that reads:

Just a little gift for you in your underwear drawer for being the best girl a guy like me could ever ask for. I love you, Sweetie

'Awww, that's so sweet,' I think. I open the drawer and count the money in the corner—ten thousand dollars. Damn, that's a hell of a gift! There is a note attached to the money that reads:

Take a week or two off work on me, my love. Crawl back into bed and wait for me to return. I love you.

I think that is the sweetest thing ever. I jump in the shower and clean the sex off my body. I put on my cute PJ's and clean my room. I change my bedding then go into the kitchen to cook; I am starving. I whip up some steak and potatoes, some Red Lobster biscuits, and grape Kool-Aid. I make a side salad and smash. I clean my kitchen and put Face's plate in the microwave.

I pull off my robe and crawl into bed. Before I can relax good, my cell phone begins to ring. It is Marko.

"Hey, baby, where are you? I'm at the bar and you're not here."

"I don't dance on the eastside every night. I told you I'm a westside rider, baby. I decided not to dance tonight; my body is a little sore from all the walking we did at the mall today. My thighs are a little weak, and you know I have to use my legs to work, baby."

"Yeah, I know, but I was really expecting to see you. I wanted to get a personal dance. I kind of miss you and all that ass."

I laugh. "All my ass? Really?"

"Now, lady, you know it was just a joke. I just miss you. What are you doing?" he asks.

"Lying in bed, watching TV."

"Can I come and lie with you tonight?"

"Not tonight. My girl has a card party going and we wouldn't be alone," I quickly answer.

"Well, you can come to me then? We'd be alone at my house, just you and me."

I sit up in my bed quickly, thinking this could be the moment I do what I need to do. I don't answer right away. I begin to think I could end this mission tonight.

"Okay, I guess I can come lie with you. Text me the info and I'll be there as soon as I slip on some clothes."

"Bring your bag. I want you to stay the night."

"Damn!" I say to myself. "Face ain't gon like this shit at all!"

I agree and end the call. I call Face to fill him in on the mission. He doesn't answer his phone so I wait as I pack my bag. I put my gun in my purse and my knife under my left breast. I don't know how I'll do it, but I plan on ending this tonight. By any means necessary, I have to kill this man. I call Face one last time, he still doesn't answer.

I'll jump in Kia's car because she has my truck blocked in. She walks me outside and I fill her in on what I'm up to. I tell her to tell Face not to call my phone. I forward the text message with Marko's address to Kia so she knows exactly where I am.

When I get to Marko's, his house is in Southfield, not on the eastside. I'm really not surprised. I knew he didn't live on the eastside; that's just where he grew up. His house is beautiful. I call his phone when I pull up and he comes to the door. I get out the car and walk up to the door with a smile on my face because he looks so damn good. I have to remind myself of the job I have to do. He is standing in the doorway in his boxers, and in his left hand he holds a silver-and-black .45. The bulge in the front of his boxers leads me to believe he is packing more than that .45. He opens the door wider for me to come in and I walk by.

"Damn, you smell good as hell!" he says.

"Thank you."

"Go to the back, down the hall, and to the right. Put your things in there. Meet me back here and I'll take you on a tour."

I do as he tells me to. Marko waits in his living room for me. As I walk toward him, my heart races. This man is fine as hell. Damn, he's making this shit hard! He takes me around his house and it is beautiful. He welcomes me and makes me feel right at home.

"Hey, follow me," he says.

I follow him down some stairs that lead to his basement. He has soft music playing, candles lit, and bottles of Moet on the built-in bar. He pours some in our glasses and make a toast, "To new beginnings."

'Wow,' I think, *'this shit right here is real.'*

Once we drink our Moet, he refills our glasses and walks me over to a room filled with candles, a Jacuzzi, and red rose petals. "Oh my gosh, Marko, this is beautiful! Ummm . . . you trying to be romantic?" I smile.

"Baby, I just think you deserve to relax. You said your muscles are hurting. Take your clothes off and get in the water. I done seen that ass and those tits before, so don't be shy."

'Damn!' I think as I set my glass down and take my clothes off.

He just stands there, looking me up and down. His package is falling out his boxers. "Damn, baby, that pussy's pretty-as-fuck!" he says as he rubs on his dick.

I'm trying to think of something to say so I can pull my knife from under my left breast. I take my drink to the head and ask for more. When he walks out, I slip my knife in my shoe. When he walks back in with my drink, he is butt naked. His dick is hung like a horse.

'Shit,' I think, *'Face is working with a lot, but this nigga's dick makes Face's dick look like a toddler's.'* This man is unreal to me. My mind goes blank as I watch him step in the water looking fabulous.

He walks over to me and pulls me into his chest. He holds my face with his hands and he kisses me so softly. I'd be lying if I said I wasn't turned on. He moves behind me and sits down, then sits me on his lap. He starts kissing my neck and massaging my shoulders. Then he puts both hands on my thighs and begins to massage them.

"How does that feel, baby? I just want to rub all of your pain away."

"That feels great." I lay my head back on his chest and relax.

Slowly his hands move on my body, one lands on my breast and the other on my pussy. He rubs my firm breast and plays with my pussy at the same time. I have to stop him. He is really turning me on.

"Marko, I'm not ready," I whisper in his ear.

"Ready for what?" he asks as he moves his fingers faster in and out my pussy. He kisses and licks all over my neck and back.

I begin to recognize this feeling my body has only felt the two times Face and I made love. I can't believe his fingers are about to send me into another world. I can't hold in the moans escaping my lips. His touch feels so good. Distracted, I cry out, "Oh my gosh, I think I'm cumming!" My legs are shaking and my pussy has a pulse. I am moaning so loud. I can't help myself. He places his fingers inside me as I squirm around on his lap. Once I release all of my juices, he pulls his fingers out of my whirlpool and sucks them dry. He lifts me up and turns me around on his lap. He tries to enter my soaked pussy with his dick.

"Wait, Marko, you don't understand! I'm a virgin."

He stops, looks at me, and chuckles. "That's why you said you *think* you're coming. You've never come before."

Acting embarrassed, I smirk and say yes. It is strange he doesn't get mad. He kisses me and says, "When I do get in that pussy, you ain't gon want nobody else to touch it."

He starts kissing me so sexily. He holds me with one arm and holds his dick in the other hand. He strokes his dick up and down as he asks me to join him by putting my hands around his dick as well. We stroke together for a minute then he moves his hands. I kiss him passionately and stroke his dick at the same time. He begins to make sex faces as he cries out in ecstasy and explodes all over my hands.

I am pleased. I got out of fucking him. I must remember my mission. I am slowly forgetting what I am here for. He steps out of the water and grabs us some towels. We dry our wet bodies then he leads me upstairs to his bedroom. I slip into my sexy PJ's and lie in the bed. He puts on *Love Jones* and joins me. We talk and watch movies until he falls asleep. I thought he was going to stay awake forever.

I slip my body from under his arm and reach for my knife I've tucked away in my shoe. He begins to move, so I roll back over with my knife in my hand. Preparing to cut his throat, I straddle him as if I am going to ride him. Looking down at him almost makes me change my mind; he is a fine piece of art and he is kind of sweet.

"The mission!" I say to myself. "Sorry, Marko, but I have a job to do," I whisper.

I open my blade and start to ease toward his throat. Just as I lean down close to his face, I hear a door slam. His eyes pop open and he scares the shit out of me. Good thing my knife is out of sight. He grabs his gun out of the nightstand and moves me off him.

"Hold on, baby, let me go check this out," he says and exits the room.

I think, *'I almost had his ass.'*

I put my knife back in my shoe and listen as he speaks to someone. I go to my bag and get my gun. Hell, I don't know who's out there. Then I hear him say, "You know you're supposed to call before you come."

"My bad, bro. I thought you were on the eastside," his little brother King responds.

As they continue their conversation, I begin to worry. I was on top of him; he probably thinks I was trying to give him some pussy. Now what am I going to do? I put my gun back in my bag and get back in bed, hoping he will be turned off and angry that his brother popped up. I am praying he'll forget I was on top of him.

When he comes back in the room, he explains how his brother stops by time-to-time with his women trying to stunt. He apologizes. When he climbs back in bed, he has that look in his eyes and I know just what it means. He gives me a kiss on my cheek, working his way around to my mouth. With his tongue, he massages mine. The kiss we share is so passionate my body begins to beg for his touch.

I play the innocent role, letting him lead the way. Wanting him inside me, I feel guilty thinking about Face. My mission has been interrupted. My plan to never let him inside has failed. My mind is all over the place. I try my best to block out that I like the way his hands feel all over my body. His kisses are sweet as sugar. He puts my breast in his mouth and nibbles on my nipple.

"Damn, baby, these are beautiful!" he says, referring to my breasts.

As he sucks, nibbles, and kisses all over them, I am quiet, but let go of soft moans from time-to-time. My body is shaking. I am scared thinking about what I will tell Face. My thoughts quickly go away as I feel his dick trying to enter my pussy. I reach down and grab his dick to check for a condom. It is there. How he managed to slip it on without me seeing is amazing to me.

Holding his dick in his hand, he slowly eases inside me. He is so much larger than Face, it hurts like hell. My pussy doesn't want to open. He uses his fingers to wet my opening by sucking them then placing them inside me. He moves his fingers in-and-out, side-to-side, until my pussy is wet like a river. Once again, he attempts to enter, this time succeeding. I let out a big moan as he forces himself inside me.

"Damn, baby, this pussy is tight! I'm about to make her familiar with my dick. She'll be my pussy when I'm done," he whispers in my ear. I just hold on to his back as he begins to move up and down. He takes long, slow strokes. "This is the introduction," he says.

He is so arrogant. He knows his dick is good and makes sure he tells me. I try my best not to enjoy myself, but it is so hard. He feels so good inside me. His body is smooth as butter. His kisses feel like small raindrops on my body, keeping me moist. Marko is in control. His slow strokes get faster. His soft hands become rough as he flips me over on my stomach so he can enter me from the back. At this time, gentle goes out the window. He grabs me by my hair and pulls me onto his dick.

"OH NO, WAIT! WAIT!" I yell out.

That only turns him on. He begins to bang me from the back, slapping my ass with one hand and holding me down by my neck with the other. Now I understand the meaning of face down, ass up. He is so deep inside me, I can feel him in my stomach. I try my best to ease away.

"Come here, girl; quit running. You're a big girl; you can take this dick!"

He slaps my ass again, lets go of my neck, and grabs my waist. He is out of control. He holds my waist as he goes in hard on my pussy. I begin to shed tears. This big-dick nigga is killing my pussy. He has no mercy. He flips me onto my back, wraps my legs around his waist, and carries me over to the wall. He places my back against the wall and holds me tight. He fucks me so good I want to scream.

"Come on, baby, fuck me back," he whispers in my ear.

I try to move along with him as I hold his neck tighter. The pain turns into pleasure as my pussy begins to swallow his dick. He holds me up by my ass cheeks as he slides one of his fingers in my ass. I damn-near jump out of his hands.

"What are you doing to me?" I cry.

"Fucking you like no man ever will," he answers. He looks up and notices I have tears in my eyes. "Oh, baby, I'm sorry. I didn't know I was hurting you. You were feeling so good to me, I lost control."

He walks me over to the bed and lays me on my back. He holds my legs in the air with his arms and enters my pussy with ease. Once inside, he loses control again. I try to hold his pelvis back to control the situation. He takes my hands and holds them down on the bed. With nowhere to run, I get fucked. I hate to admit it . . . but I like it.

When Marko is ready to cum, he pulls out, snatches his condom off, and busts all over my body. My pussy is hurting, but it feels so good. He smacked it up, flipped it, and rubbed it down. Oh, he is such a good fuck. Confused, I lie there, once again thinking of Face. I know my pussy will tell on me if I let Face near it any time soon. This big-dick nigga busted my shit wide open. When it is all over, we lie there breathing hard. I can feel fluids running down my leg. I get up and go to the bathroom in his bedroom. I look down at my leg and blood is everywhere. This nigga fucked me like I am a hoe.

I turn on the shower and jump in, letting the hot water wash away the dirt I've allowed on my body. I begin to think how fucked up I've made this situation. Face never returned my call so I don't know how he's going to feel about this sleepover. My thoughts are interrupted by Marko when he joins me in the shower. He stands behind me and washes my back.

"Are you mad at me?"

"No, I'm not mad."

He turns me around so that we are face-to-face and kisses me softly. "She'll never forget me," he whispers.

"I don't want her to," I respond.

We wash our bodies and get out the shower. I oil my body while Marko changes the sheets and covers on the bed. Once we're done, we lie in the bed and he falls asleep. Morning can't come soon enough. Once I see daylight, I get up and prepare to leave.

"Baby, where are you going?" Marko asks.

"I have business to handle."

I get my things together and head towards the door. Marko walks me out. Once we get to the living room, I see his little brother King sitting on the couch.

"Hey, shorty, I see you finally made it this way," King says, trying to be funny.

I just look at that nigga sideways. His ass had better be easy or I'll get him, too. I walk out and jump in the ride. My mind is running and my pussy is hurting. My heart is feeling some type of way. As much as I love Face, I can't believe I betrayed him. Did I do what I had to do to complete this mission? I feel bad about the night I've shared with Marko. Truth be told, I enjoyed him and every moment we shared.

Chapter 9 ✳ Mission Complete

I find out Face is locked up. I have been calling since I got home from my night out. I thought he was angry about me spending the night with Marko; come to find out, he never knew. He calls me and I have to go bail him out. I don't mention my night with Marko. On the ride home, we talk about why he was arrested. He got pulled over for speeding and they took him in for an old warrant he skipped out on years ago.

"I tried to call you to tell you thanks for the gift you left in my drawer."

"You know you're good for whatever you want, baby. You're my right hand. Shit, I need you to function!"

I smile. Face always expresses his love for me with no problem. This man loves me and I know it. That's why I have to end this mess with Marko.

"Well, I kind of have good news," I say.

"Oh yeah? What's that?"

"Marko wants me to come to his house. Once we see where he lives, maybe I can fall back and y'all can get his ass."

He agrees. "I don't like the thought of that nigga breathing on you. You go; make sure you peep the whole house so we can hit his ass right. But don't let that nigga touch you!" Face says, looking grim as hell.

"I feel you, baby," I say, looking out the window. I can't look him in his face and act like I didn't just fuck that nigga last night.

Maybe if I hadn't liked it, I wouldn't feel so bad. "That nigga's gotta go. It's kind of too much; he's getting to the point where he wants to be touchy-feely. I figure when I get over there I'll have on a pair of my period panties," I lie.

I want Face to feel secure. I want him to believe he can trust me. Truthfully, I don't want to spend any more time with Marko, so I really want to handle my business tonight. I just hope King's ass doesn't show up.

I take Face to get his car out of the impound. He kisses me and says he has to make some moves. He tells me to text him when I'm ready leave to meet up with that bitch-ass nigga. If it's possible, we're gon try to hit his ass tonight. I tell Face I need a rental car. I don't want my truck anywhere near the area. He tells me to handle my business. He'll pick up a rental car that can't be traced.

"I love you, baby," I say.

"I love you more," he responds and we part ways.

I ride home nervous as hell. I really don't want Face to find out about my fucking session with Marko. I go home and prepare myself for the night. My heart is in my shoes. "I'm not a killer. What the fuck am I doing?" I ask myself. Face is the only man who has ever protected me. I love him more than me.

The time has come. Marko calls me to tell me he is home waiting for me to arrive. I text Face to tell him I'm headed out. I give him Marko's address and cross streets, just in case I can't get the job done. I jump in my truck and go to the location Face has parked the rental. His boy June takes my truck and I leave.

I pull up at Marko's house and get out. I have my knife under my boob and my gun in my bag. I ring the doorbell and he opens the door right away.

"Damn, did you know who it was?" I ask.

"I saw you walking up."

My mind is racing; I know what I've come to do. We walk in the dining room, and sit down and talk for a minute.

"I thought you would never come back after our last encounter," Marko says.

"Well, why would you think that?"

I stand up and walk toward him, straddle him, and begin to kiss all over him. I inhale slowly while kissing him. He smells so good. He put his arms around me and places his hands on my ass. He kisses me back with so much passion, rubbing his hands up and down my body, my pussy is calling for him. I must admit I'm getting a rush thinking about fucking him then killing him.

"I knew you would love it. That pussy's been begging for me, hasn't she?"

I hate how arrogant he is. I want to spit in his face. I want him to take my pussy, but I hate him, too. His dick begins to rise. I have on a cute little dress and a sexy thong. Marko plays with my clit as we kiss and grind on one another. He picks me up and carries me into his room. He places me on the bed then lifts my dress.

"I'm about to make you love me," he whispers.

He starts at my thighs and moves up slowly; with one finger, he pulls my G-string over to the side, and with his tongue, he satisfies me. I can't stop my knees from shaking and I can't control my body wanting him to please me more. I know he wants me just as much as I want him. He pulls my panties off, spreading my legs wide open. He climbs on top of me and slides inside my whirlpool. Soaking wet, my pussy welcomes him in. I let out a moan of pleasure and pain; loving how he feels inside me, I pull him in deeper.

"Oh, you trying to handle this dick today? Baby, is it good to you?"

"Yes, baby, it's good."

Marko is so different from Face. His smooth-but-rough edges are such a turn-on to me. He's older than Face and his sex game is so much better, not to mention the size of his dick. It is hard to keep my mind on the mission when he puts his hands on me. Face has my heart, but right now, Marko's dick has my mind, body, and damn-near my soul. Yes, all of that happens after one hit. This nigga puts it down.

Round two is the best I've ever had. I know I have to kill his ass, or else I'll keep coming back for more. Marko is nasty with his sex. He's pulling his dick out, sucking my pussy, then putting it back in. He flips me over and eats it from the back. He's pulling my hair, slapping my ass, and sucking on my fingers. He fucks me like he owns the pussy. I give it to him like it's his.

When he puts me on top and tells me to ride his dick, I learn that riding is my favorite position. I sit on his dick and move in a circular motion. Looking him in his eyes, I tell him to tell me how much he enjoys my pussy.

"I'll show you how much," Marko says as he grabs me by my waist, picks me up, and sits me on his face. It feels like he is sucking the insides out of my pussy. He has me gone. I scream out in ecstasy.

"Marko, I'm cumming!"

He snatches me off his face and places me back on his dick. Grinding his hips up and down slow but hard, he fucks me so good I want to suck my thumb. He lets out a groan and I know he's cumming all inside me. Once he lets my ass go, I collapse on his chest, feeling so weak I can't think of my next move. Damn, I wanna keep this man for myself. It's just sex with us, but it's *great* sex. I know I will probably never be fucked like this again.

"I'm sorry I didn't pull out. I was caught up in the moment," Marko says.

"Whatever! You just wanna be my baby-daddy," I say as I chuckle.

"Shit! You got that type of pussy a nigga don't wanna come out of."

"I wonder how many hoes you done told that same shit," I say with my mouth twisted up.

"Baby, I don't have any children out here; I don't fuck raw. Just knowing I was your first piece made me a little comfortable in the pussy. For some reason, I think of it as mine."

I just smile, climb off him, and grab my purse. I go into the bathroom to freshen up. "SO ARE WE JUST GOING TO BE FUCK-BUDDIES, OR ARE WE GOING TO HAVE A RELATIONSHIP?" I yell out the bathroom.

"Baby, I'm feeling you, but I told you from the start, I'm not looking to settle down. I just wanna have fun, and if it goes there, we'll handle it when we get to that point."

"Oh, so you fuck other bitches and I only fuck you. Is that how it's going to go?" I ask with an attitude.

"Bae, why're you mad? I told you up front how I am. I've never been in love and I don't have any plans on falling in love, but if it happens with you and me, then it happens."

I peek out the bathroom, and this nigga is smiling, stroking his dick, and talking about, "Good boy; I knew you were going to make her love you. Now she's hooked."

Everything I think about this nigga flies out the window. The look on his face disgusts me. He got just what he wanted from me, so I have to get what I want from him—his last breath. I pull my gun out of my purse and check the chamber. I make sure he doesn't hear me check by talking over the noise.

"Wow! So I'm just another hit under your belt," I say.

"My boys don't call me Mr. Hit Man for nothing, baby."

I come out the bathroom mad as hell. It is Face's war, but it has become my fight and I refuse to lose. His eyes pop wide open when he sees my gun pointed at his head.

"Your thirst for this pussy has made you, the untouchable man, easy to be touched. You bitch! Mission complete!" I say, right before I put a bullet straight through his head.

My heart is pounding as I grab his cellphone, money, and jewelry, and put it in my purse. I clean up everything I've touched, even his dick, covered with my juices. I pick up my panties off the floor and head for the door. I open the door and I'm shocked his boy Joe is standing right in front of me.

"What's up, pretty lady? Where's Marko?"

I exhale, shaking because this nigga has changed my plans. "He's in the back," I say as I act like I was leaving out. He walks down the hall towards Marko's room. I watch as I close the front door softly.

"YO, MARKO!" Joe yells out.

"Hey, Joe," I call out.

"What's up?" Joe asks as he turns around, only to see my loaded pistol looking back at him.

"He's sleep," I say before letting go five shots to his head and body.

I run out the door, jump in my car, and take off slowly. I don't want the neighbors to look outside if they haven't already. I call Face so his boy can bring me my truck. I don't say a word about what just happened. I just say, "You know I love you."

"I love you, too," Face says.

"Okay, I'll see you soon."

I make the switch, jump in my truck, and head home. I really don't feel anything. I am numb. Hell, in the end, I killed him for me. I fucked around and got my feelings hurt. His boy Joe was just at the wrong place at the wrong time. Pussy is a bad muthafucka. I can't believe he trusted me to come to his main spot. That's what made me think he was feeling me. He must have thought this sweet little striper could do him no harm. Oh well, I just saved a lot of hoes from getting their little hearts broken by Mr. Marko, the Untouchable.

When I get home Face, Kia, and Stone are sitting at the dining room table. All eyes are on me when I walk in.

"You okay, boo," Kia asks.

"Yeah, I'm good," I say as I walk into the bathroom. I turn on the shower and take off my clothes. It is at that very moment I realize what I have done. I've killed a man who really didn't do anything to me. My love for another man has turned me into a heartless murderer.

I stand in the shower and let the water beat on my back. My face is covered with water that helps hide the tears I let fall. I thought this would be easy. I killed two men before and never gave a fuck. I guess it was because they'd hurt me. This man actually made me feel good; I am so confused. I stay in the shower until the water is cold.

Face comes into the bathroom. "Bae, are you okay?"

"He's dead. I had to kill his friend, too."

"All that matters is you got out safely," Face says.

He pulls me out the shower and wraps a towel around me. Then he walks me to my bedroom. I climb my naked body into bed and fall asleep. Face stays by my side the whole night. When we wake up, it is all over the news.

"Kingpin Prince Marko was found dead in his Southfield home. His friend Joe Wills was also shot several times inside the home as well. Neighbors say they heard several gunshots then saw a small black car leaving the scene. No suspects or leads at this time. We will keep you updated as we get more information," the newscaster says.

Face and I look at one another with big eyes. We don't say a word. My body feels crazy. My heart is pounding; this shit is real. I hope I didn't leave any evidence behind. I think I cleaned up well.

"Where's the car I drove?" I ask Face.

"Bae, don't worry about that car. It's on its way to Florida. Keys sold that car to a girl who just moved there. He's delivering it to her as we speak. The plate isn't registered so you have nothing to worry about."

Things were already crazy; now things are worse. I have killed two men for the love of one. Shit, is it really love? Maybe it's just plain crazy.

Chapter 10 ✳ King's Revenge

It's been three months since my brother's death, and I swear I'm losing my mind. My brother and I were tight. He taught me everything I know. He was my best friend and I miss him like crazy. I've been hitting the streets hard as hell trying to find out who did that shit. A bitch had to have set him up. They found him butt-naked in his bed. It's just strange. Joe was found in the hallway that leads to Marko's bedroom. I can't help but wonder if he was setting Marko up and his partner blazed his ass. Then I think maybe he walked in on the shit.

I sit around all day trying to put the shit together. I haven't found shit yet. Whoever did it took his money and jewelry. I've been to several pawn shops, showing pictures of his shit and none of them has seen it yet. I haven't been out at all since my brother died. Tonight will be my first night out. I'm going to hit a couple of strip clubs to see if anyone has heard anything. One thing I know fo' sho is bitches love to run their mouths.

I don't go by myself. I have to go deep. The person who killed my brother could be looking for me, that's why I'm on the lookout at all times. The first bar I hit is an eastside titty bar. Marko didn't go to clubs. He hated niggas, and the only way he would tolerate them was at a titty bar. Going to different bars will allow me to see how niggas and bitches are acting. My goons are ready for war. I hit a few bars on the east and things appear to be the same. I am looking for a girl Marko had just started fucking with, but I can't find her. I ask a couple of questions, but no one knows shit.

I head west. I go to the bars I know he went to the most. The first bar I hit, as soon as I walk in, she's coming to the stage. Storm, that's her name. She's the last bitch he was fucking with. He was feeling her ass, too. Marko would let me fuck any other bitch he hit, but not her. He told me up front she was off limits. I need to talk to her to see what's up.

I have on all-black because I don't really want to stand out. I have my hood pulled all the way down over my forehead. I am on some low-key shit. Storm is working the stage, popping that big-ass booty all over the place. I walk up to the stage and throw a bunch of twenties at her. She looks at me and winks. I pull my hood back, exposing my face. She winks again and keeps dancing. I guess she knows it's me. I put my hood on and walk over to our favorite corner.

I see Storm's girl Thunder working the floor. I call her over to do a personal dance; she comes right over and gets to work. She smells so good. Her ass is so soft and pretty. She has me in a trance as she dances. She is doing the damn thang. She leans over my shoulder and whispers in my ear.

"How are you, sweetie?"

"I'm good, baby doll; just taking it slow," I answer.

She finishes her dance, kisses me on my forehead, and walks away. I stay 'til the bar closes to be able to talk to Storm.

"Hey, what's up? Why haven't you been to the east?" I ask.

"Why would I come east? I was only there because Marko wanted me there," she answers.

"Have you heard anything about what happened to him?" I ask her.

"Just what they've reported on the news, nothing else. How're you holding up?" she asks with a sideways grin. Maybe I'm just tripping.

"I've been good, ma; just looking for my brother's killer. When I find out who did the shit, I'm going to take their muthafuckin head off. Real talk," I say, mad as fuck.

"Well, I gotta go. You take care," she says as she walks off.

My mind is all over the place. Why would she want Marko dead? She had no reason to kill him. He would have given her the world and she knew that. Fuck it, though; everyone is suspect until I find out who did that shit.

I go home with a lot on my mind. I can't sleep so I pace the floor all night. I am pissed because I didn't accomplish shit at the bars I hit. I have to make sure I'm not next. I have to admit this is the first time I've been scared for my life. We were known as the Untouchables for a reason. Who the hell had the balls to go in his house and take his life like that?

Another month has passed and I finally start to get info about the night Marko was killed. People hadn't noticed that the news reported Marko's boy Joe was shot as well but they never said he was dead. He's been on life support and he just woke up. I am heading to see his ass. He'd better be saying some shit I wanna hear or I'll finish his ass.

When I get to the hospital, Joe's whole family is there celebrating. I wait patiently. When they all clear out, I walk in.

"What's up, Joe? I'm so happy you came back, man. How're you feeling?" I ask.

"He can't talk, King. The bullet that hit him in the neck is still there," Joe's girlfriend says.

"DAMN!" I yell out.

Joe grabs a pen and pad, and holds it in the air so I can see it. That shit makes me smile.

"Who did this to y'all?" I ask.

He writes on the pad the word 'stripper'.

"STRIPPER!" I yell.

He writes "yes" on the pad. I start to tremble. "What's her name? Was she alone? How did she get in?"

"Slow down, King. He's not a hundred percent better yet. Give him time to write," his girl says.

"MY BAD, DAMN! I NEED TO KNOW WHO DID THE SHIT. FOR HIS SAFETY AND MINE. SHIT, THEY MIGHT BE COMING BACK!" I yell.

Joe takes the pen and writes, "The real pretty stripper, brown skin, big butt, and long hair."

"If I bring you a picture, will you be able to point her out?" I ask Joe.

He writes 'yes'.

I have a new mission. I'm not sure how I'm going to work this shit, but I promise Joe I will be back with pictures. I wish he could have narrowed it down for me. I'll just start with the ones I know he fucked for sure. I have a long night ahead of me. All the boys are ready to party because Joe made it through. I, on the other hand, don't give a fuck. I want to get the muthafucka who killed my brother. I'm not stopping until it's done.

It's ride time and I am about to ride for mine. I hit every spot I can think of. I spend all kinds of money on bitches. I take pictures with every bitch I even *think* that nigga fucked with. Everyone acts normal to me. I hit the eastside first then I head west. I do the same thing on the west. I spend money, buy drinks, and take pictures all night.

I am looking for Storm but she isn't around. Her girl Thunder is in the building. I'm not sure if she's avoiding me or if she's just extra busy. I can't get her to come my way so I can't get a good picture of her. I snap a quick picture of her while she's working the stage. I'll catch her girl later. I'm tired as fuck and I want to get up early to go to the hospital. I tell all the boys I'm ready to bounce and we leave.

I get home and lie across the bed. I toss and turn the whole time, never closing my eyes. I cry just thinking about Marko. I wish it was me gone because my heart can't take this pain.

"I AM GOING TO KILL THE PERSON WHO DID THIS TO YOU, BRO, OR I'LL DIE TRYING!" I yell out loud.

Morning is staring me in the face. I jump up, brush my teeth, and head to the hospital in the same clothes I had on the night before. I mean business. I am the first one to arrive at the hospital. When

I walk in, Joe is up, trying to eat. He looks better than he did the yesterday.

"What's up, Joe-Joe?" I ask as I enter the room.

He gives me the thumbs up.

"I have these pictures for you to look at," I say.

Joe motions for me to give him the pictures. I took about sixty pictures last night. I pass the pictures to Joe and watch as he begins to go through them. He is almost done and still hasn't picked one. My hands begin to shake. I am so ready to handle a bitch, I don't know what to do. Joe passes me the photos back, shaking his head.

"None of these hoes, Joe?" I ask. He shakes his head no. "BITCH!" I say, loud as fuck.

I jump up and start pacing the floor, shaking my head back and forth. I am pissed! My phone starts to ring, and just as I start to answer it, I remember Thunder's picture is in my phone. I push "end" on the call and pull up my photo gallery. I pull up the picture of Thunder and pass my phone to Joe.

"Is it her?" I ask Joe.

Joe eyes opened wide as he hits the picture with his pointer finger. "Her, nigga? She the one?" I ask again.

Joe shakes his head no. Pointing to the table, he asks for his pen and pad. I hand it to him, and he writes on the pad and passes it back to me. The pad says, 'It was her girl. Not sure what her name is, but I am sure it was her girl.'

I ball the paper up and begin to shake. "STORM! THAT BITCH! I KNEW IT WAS HER. WHY THE FUCK WOULD SHE DO THAT SHIT?" I yell.

Tears begin to roll down my face. The anger in my heart makes me feel like I am about to explode. "I can't wait to catch that bitch. I am going to snap her pretty little neck," I say.

Joe wrote on the pad. "She's cold-blooded, bro. She looked me in my eyes and shot me five times. Be careful, nigga. Don't sleep on that bitch. She's got to be an assassin."

I give Joe a funny look. "Nigga, I wouldn't care if the bitch was the president. Her ass is good as dead. I'm out, Joe. I'll holla at you later," I say.

Happy I have the info I need, I fly out the hospital, ready to kill. I call my boys and put them up on game. I make sure I tell them I want to be the one to kill her. I wanna look her in her eyes and watch her die. I tell my main man Ice to meet me at the bar she dances at on a regular because I'm killing that bitch tonight. I don't need a fuckin' plan; that bitch has to die and that is that.

Later that night, we go to the bar. I don't smoke or drink. I have to be one hundred. I send my boy in the bar to see if she's in there. When he comes out, he has a look on his face I don't like.

"I didn't see her," he says as he walks up to my car.

"FUCK!" I yell.

The bar is about to close, so I figure she is in the back getting dressed. I sit in the parking lot and wait for all the dancers to come out. The night I popped up at Marko's house, she was driving a blue Honda. I look around the parking lot, and bam! There it is. I am on chill mode until this bitch comes out the bar. The parking lot is just about clear.

I never see Storm, but her girl comes out, jumps in the car, and pulls off. I follow her. I am just about sure she'll lead us to her girl. I did do a little research, and word on the street is they are roommates. I leave the lot right behind her. She never pays me any attention; I have my boys on both sides of her car to distract her. She is so busy watching them, she never sees me.

Once they turned off different ways, we are all alone. I have my headlights off and I am driving my car we all call the ghost. It is all-black everything. If the headlights are off, you can't see this bitch in the dark. She drives like she has no worries. Dumb bitch never looks back.

"Take me to your friend, you stupid hoe," I say aloud.

She pulls in the driveway of this big-ass house. "Bingo!" I say as I notice Storm's Range Rover in the driveway. Thunder walks her happy ass to the door. She's looking around now.

"It's too late for that shit, baby girl," I whisper.

I watch as she puts her keys in the door. I get out of my car, sneak up behind her, and as she opens the door, I grab her around her neck and cover her mouth with my hand. I don't want her to scream, knowing her girl is a cold shooter. I don't want her to be aware of the danger that is near.

"Shut the fuck up, hoe. I'm going to uncover your mouth and you're going to call for your girl Storm. You'd better sound regular, too, or I'll snap your fuckin' neck," I say.

"Fuck you, nigga. You might as well snap my neck 'cause I'll never betray my friend. I'll die first, bitch!"

I almost give the bitch some respect for being so loyal. Some niggas ain't even as loyal as this bitch. I give Little Jay the signal to come inside. "Hey, check all the rooms," I say to Jay.

I hold Thunder tight and kick the front door shut with my foot. I can't believe how calm this bitch is. She isn't even breathing heavy. She shows no fear.

"King, ain't nobody in this bitch. I checked all the rooms," Jay says.

I am so angry I can feel my blood boil. I begin to shake. My grip gets loose and Thunder gets free. She turns around and sprays me with mace. She tries to make it to her bag but Jay grabs her by her ponytail. She sprays his ass, too. This bitch isn't going down easy. I am coughing and rubbing my eyes, and Lil Jay is doing the same. She gets to her bag, pulls out a Mag, and starts busting. I hear Jay scream, "I'M HIT."

I'm still trying to clean my eyes and catch my breath. I fall to the floor, hoping she can't see me. Still trying to catch my breath, I lie still and listen to her move around. She must think we were both dead, or hit. I clear my eyes one last time, and I see her heading for the door. Just as she gets there, I let off two shots and listen as she hits the floor.

I get up, looking for Jay. Somehow, he'd gotten out the house and is laid out by my car. I open the door and put him in the car. I am still having trouble seeing, but we have to leave. I take off doing sixty down the block.

"I got that bitch. I don't know where, but I know I got her ass," I say to Jay. "That bitch was a fighter. Now I know what I am up against when I catch her girl."

I kind of wish I hadn't done things this way. Now the bitch is gon be on the lookout. She could try to come for me, or she'll hide. These are some different type of bitches.

I drop Jay off at the hospital and his girl meets him up there. I'm not staying around for shit. I feel fucked-up when I get home. I ain't never killed a girl, and never thought I would have to. Truth of the matter is, at this point I could kill anybody. I won't stop until that bitch, Storm, is a sleeping beauty.

"I promise you, bro," I say out loud. I lie down and sleep wide awake. That's how deep this shit is.

"Until we meet again, Storm," I whisper.

Chapter 11 ✴ Rude Awakening

Things have been so crazy these last four months. After I finally get over the two murders I've committed, I begin to live again. Face and I have been in Vegas for the last week, and now we are headed home. I needed this vacation so bad. We had a ball. We partied, made love, and stayed drunk the whole time. Vegas is beautiful and I plan to come back.

We leave the room at noon headed to the airport. Our plane is set to take off at two p.m. I call Kia to let her know what time to pick us up but she doesn't answer. I'll call her again once we check in at the airport. We arrive at the airport and check in. We grab something to eat and a couple of drinks. We sit around talking shit and laughing about our trip until it's time to board the plane.

I call Kia again and still no answer. I begin to worry. We are told to turn our phones off when it's time for takeoff.

"That's weird," I say to Face.

"Yeah, she must have lost her phone or something," Face says.

"Even if she did, she would have called me by now somehow."

I try my best not to worry. I close my eyes and sit back in my seat. When I open my eyes, we are back in the D. We get off the plane and head to baggage claim. We get our bags and head to the pickup area. Once we get outside and notice Kia isn't outside, I get scared. Now I know something is wrong. Face calls Stone and asks him if he has heard from Kia. He says no and he has been trying to call her since late last night. Face ends the call, we jump in a cab, and head to my house.

When we pull up to my house, without thinking, I jump out the car and run into the house. Kia's car is in the driveway and the front door is wide open.

"WAIT, REA, DON'T JUST GO IN!" Face yells as he jumps out the cab.

I don't give a fuck! I run in anyway. I scream loudly and fall to my knees at the sight of my best friend, my only friend, lying dead behind the front door. I grab Kia up in my arms and hold her as I scream, "NO, NO, NO! LORD, PLEASE HELP ME! HELP ME!" I cry out.

Face drops all our bags in the yard as he runs in to help me. "WHAT THE FUCK! WHAT THE FUCK!" Face yells.

"SHE'S GONE, FACE! SHE'S GONE. MY FRIEND IS GONE. MY SISTER, MY EVERYTHING—SHE'S GONE! SOMEBODY KILLED HER!" I cry.

Face calls the police then tries to pry my hands off Kia's body. I refuse to let her go. "Kia, who did this to you? Who?" I cry.

Tears run down my face like a waterfall. My nose is running like a baby's. Snot is everywhere. I hold Kia's dead body in my arms until the police make me let her go. I sit in Kia's blood while the police question me. I tell them all I can. I really don't know much; I wasn't even in town. I begin to scan the house for clues, looking around to see if anything is missing. Police are everywhere.

Kia's bag is next to the wall she died by. On the side of her bag, written in her blood, are the letters K, I, N, and a letter that looks as if it was going to be a G.

"King," I whisper.

I begin to cry harder, thinking about my girl lying here dying, and yet, she was protecting me. I slide my foot across the wall to smear the blood. Prison won't be King's final destination, death will. I have a new mission, and his name is King. When the police clear us to leave, I grab some pictures off the fireplace and put them in a bag.

"Come here, baby; I need to show you something," I called out to Face. I show him the wall where I smeared the blood. I whisper in his ear, "King!" This shit is fucked up. My girl is dead, and it's my fuckin' fault. Face just stares at the ceiling. "Let's get the fuck outta here," Face says as he grabs my arm.

His truck is parked in the field next to my house. We jump in the truck and pull off.

"KING DID THIS, BABY. THAT NIGGA KILLED MY GIRL. HE MUST KNOW I KILLED HIS BROTHER. BUT HOW? HE WAS THERE LOOKING FOR ME!" I yelled.

Face calls Stone and tells him the terrible news. His screams are so loud I can hear him through the phone. "Who man? Who the fuck killed my baby? She can't be gone, man. Face, tell me she ain't gone," Stone cries.

Face just drops his head. Hearing Stone cry out makes me start again. "She's gone, Stone. I am so sorry, man, but she's gone. Meet me at Cuddy's house. We have some business to handle," Face says.

We take fifty different turns to Cuddy's house, Face says just to be safe. He makes sure no one is following us. When we get to Cuddy's house, all of Face's boys are there. When we walk in, everyone starts hugging me and asking if I'm okay. My tears are never going to stop. I am a mess. I am hurting so bad I don't want to breathe.

"I wish it was me. They were looking for me!" I say.

"HOW THE FUCK DID THAT NIGGA FIND OUT STORM DID THE HIT?" Face yells.

"Shit, word in the streets is that nigga Joe ain't die. He's been on life support all this time. When he came to, he remembered what happened. They say King is going ham in the streets. He's got a hundred thousand on Storm's head, dead or alive," Ronnie says.

"Damn, I shot that nigga five times! Once in the fuckin' head! I knew it! I *am* the reason she's dead!" I say.

"Fuck all the dumb shit, nigga. Send Storm away and let's go get his bitch-ass," Carl says.

"I'm down with that! I'm killing every nigga moving!" Stone says as he walks into the house. His eyes are bloodshot-red. He has a gallon of Remy in his hand and a blunt in his mouth. Rage is all in his eyes. "I don't give a fuck what happens. King's bitch-ass is mine. I'm going to chop his dick off and make him suck it, since he's a bitch!" Stone says as he pours himself a drink.

"We can't go in all dumb. These niggas are ready for whatever. Believe me, it's word, my nigga, but we gotta do this shit right! We can't leave nobody breathing. We don't need anybody looking for us when this is done," Ronny says.

"Face, send Storm back to Vegas. That nigga wants her dead or alive; as long as she's gone, he's out looking. As long as he's out looking, he's touchable," Carl says.

"I AIN'T GOING NOWHERE UNTIL I BURY MY GIRL. I AIN'T SCARED OF DEATH. AS FAR AS I'M CONCERNED, I'M ALREADY DEAD!" I yell.

"Okay, cool. We'll all be at the funeral; we just have to keep a close watch. Just like the streets are feeding us, it's going to feed them, too. If they're disrespectful, they're coming. If they're smarter than they look, they'll stay on the fuckin eastside," Pete says.

"THIS SHIT JUST GOT REAL. THEY AIN'T TAKING MY GIRL!" Face yells.

"But they killed mine! Fuck that nigga, King, and his dead brother! His ass has gotta go!" Stone cries.

We all go our separate ways. Our next meeting will be at Kia's homegoing. The week is long and stressful for me. Looking back over my life, I realize karma has finally caught up with me.

The day has come for me to bury my best friend. My heart hurts so badly. My tears are nonstop. Walking up to that casket, knowing that my sister, my best friend, my everything, will be sleeping there forever brings me to my knees. I fall to the floor right in front of the casket. Face picks me up and holds me in his arms.

"No, no, no! I need you, Kia! Please come back to me!" I cry as I stand over the casket, looking in her face. She lies there stiff but still beautiful, looking like a Barbie doll. My tears cover her face. "I know you would kill me if you knew I was messing up your makeup," I say as I laugh at the thought of hearing her say, "Girl my face is beat." I smile. "I love you, girl. They gon pay for this, or I'll pay with my life. I love you forever," I whisper before I kiss her and walk away.

My big black hat is pulled down over my face and Face stays by my side the whole time.

During the service, Stone refuses to view Kia's body. He says he just can't take it. Just as the funeral director begins to close the casket, Stone runs up front, yelling and crying, "MY BABY, MY BABY! I WISH I HAD BEEN THERE TO PROTECT YOU! I WISH I HAD BEEN THERE TO HOLD YOU. HOW COULD THIS HAPPEN? WHY? WHY?" he cries. He damn-near pulls her body out the casket. The director tries to pull Stone away. "GET THE FUCK OFF ME, NIGGA!" Stone yells. It takes Face and four of their boys to get him calm and walk him outside.

People stand up and stare as well as shedding major tears. This has to be the worse day of my life. Kia always said, when she died to cremate her because she didn't want bugs eating her beautiful body. I make sure that is taken care of. A week after the service, the ashes are ready. I have a locket made in the shape of a B that stands for best friend. I have them fill it with Kia's ashes. I attach the locket to my best friend's necklace and I promise to never remove it from my neck.

"I will wear this forever, best friend," I whisper.

All is done and Kia is resting in peace. Face drives me to the airport and off to Vegas I go.

Chapter 12 ✳ The Call

The hood has been so quiet since Kia's murder. Stone has been on the nut. Anyone who looks like he or she knows something, he's on his or her ass. I didn't know how much he loved Kia. Hell, he has a whole family in Ohio. He just told me he'd planned to leave ol' girl because he found out his son isn't his. I'm his right-hand man, and I can't believe he's just now telling me this shit. His anger is coming from so many places. My dude is out here fucked up.

I've been lying low. These niggas don't know shit. They ain't gon see us coming. I just can't wait for this shit to be over. I miss my girl. We call each other all day every day, and sometimes we fall asleep on the phone. I've made plans to fly out this Friday. I'll stay all weekend then it's back to the D for me. Storm can't come back until King's ass is dead. I feel so fucked up. I should have killed Marko myself. I let Storm and the boys make a decision I should have made. I feel responsible for all this heartache and pain. I am feeling fucked up so I need to go talk to my mother. She always makes me feel better.

Stone texts me and asks me to give him the keys to Storm's crib. He wants to look around and get some pictures he and Kia took together. I make a detour and meet him at the house. I pull up and he's just sitting in his truck.

"What's up, my nigga?" I ask as I walk up.

"Shit, man! I miss her so much. I just don't know how to get over this shit. King's ass is in hiding right now, but his hoe-ass can't hide forever," Stone says.

"Man, I feel so responsible for this bullshit."

"Man, we all sat there and planned that shit. We were drunk and mad at the same time. None of us were thinking right."

"You're right. I just don't know what else to say or do. I have never seen you hurt like this before. When your father died, you didn't even cry."

Stone looks at me with tears in his eyes. "My father wasn't a man; he was a monster. I cried all my tears when he was alive. You've been my right-hand man since then. If I've never told you before, I love you, man."

"I love you, too, my nigga."

We hug and I bounce. I still need to see my mom. I ride with my music banging, thinking about my life. I wish I could do it all over again, and I begin to shake my head. I look at myself in the mirror and picture the old me, the face I had before Marko and his boys shot me up. Rage begins to fill my body.

"Nigga, you tried to kill me over a bitch. Ha! That's why my bitch killed you!" I say out loud as I smirk at my ugly face in the mirror.

When I get to my mother's house, I walk right in. I've always had keys to her place. "Mom," I call out. It is strange for her not to answer. Her car is in the driveway. I look down the basement and she isn't there either. "Where the hell can she be?"

I call her cell phone, but still no answer. I don't panic. I make me a plate of spaghetti and turn on the TV. I assume she's gone to bingo with one of her friends. I fall asleep, and when I wake up, it's ten p.m. My mom still hasn't come home. I have five missed calls and none of them are from her. Storm has called twice so I call her back just to chat for a while. She just wants to hear my voice and tell me she loves me. She's really lonely and wants to come home. I explain to her it's best she stay where she's safe, and we say our goodbyes.

My mind starts to fuck with me. My mom has never done this shit before. I pay her cell bill so I can keep track of her. She always answers. I look in her phone book she keeps on her TV stand. I call a few of her close friends; none of them have heard from her. My heart begins to race. I sit down and close my eyes. Thirty minutes later, I receive a call from my mom's number.

"Hello, Mother, where are you?" I say playfully.

"Naw, nigga, this ain't your mommy. This is King and I wanna play let's make a deal. Now a little bird to me the bitch who killed my brother belongs to you. That same bird told me you would do anything for your mother. With that being said, I am sure you want your mother back safe and sound. You can have that, but only if you bring me the girl. Dead, nigga! I want you to kill her. I can't believe you sent your bitch to get fucked just so you didn't have to be a real nigga and kill him yourself. Now you have a problem. If you don't deliver that bitch to me in forty-eight hours, your mother will be dead."

"Baby, I'm an old lady. I'm not scared of death, so you know what I am saying. I love you, son," my mom says into the phone before it's snatched away from her. Hearing my mother's voice sends chills through my soul.

"You have forty-eight hours, nigga. Go get that bitch and bring her to me," King says before he ends the call.

I start yelling. I can't believe this nigga's got my mom. Who the fuck told him about my mom? It has to be somebody close to me. I don't know what to do. I know I need to move fast. I don't know who to call, who to trust. My time has already started. I jump in my truck and go to Storm's place, hoping Stone is still there. When I pull up, his truck is in the driveway. I call his cell phone. I don't want to just walk in. He is on one and he will shoot my ass if I scare him.

"Hello," Stone answers.

"It's me, nigga. Open the door!" I say franticly. I walk in the house with swollen, red eyes.

"What's wrong, man?" Stone asks.

"MAN, THEY'VE GOT MY MOM," I yell.

"WHO'S GOT YOUR MOM?" Stone yells.

"King, and I got forty-eight hours to bring Storm to him or he'll kill my mom. I need to find this nigga and I ain't got a lot of time. Somebody close is talking. WE'VE GOT A SNITCH ON OUR TEAM AND THEY TOLD HIM WHERE TO FIND MY MOM!" I yell.

Stone jumps up and grabs a bag of pictures. "Let's go. We ain't saying shit to nobody. We gotta do this shit ourselves!".

We dart out the door. I jump in my truck and Stone jumps in his. "HEY, FOLLOW ME. WE'RE GOING EAST," he yells out his window as he pulls up alongside me.

I follow Stone as he drives into King's territory. We are playing with fire. We will most definitely be outnumbered but we have to do what we have to do. I have two AK47's and my .45. I'm not sure what Stone is packing but I know he's *been* ready for this war. We hit King's favorite spot. We ask some of the dancers about him. Some give good info; others are loyal to his bum-ass and they refuse to talk. One bitch, Lisa, hates him as much as we do. She offers to take us to his main spot. She jumps in my ride and takes us straight to it.

"Now King comes here during the day to check on his money. If and when he comes at night, he stays till morning," Lisa says.

I know Lisa from the westside. She has been plotting on King for a while now; she believes King killed her little brother. We sit at the corner of the block and watch as niggas go in and out. King never shows up. That means he has my mom with him and he's guarding her. We drop Lisa off at her car and go back to the westside. My phone is blowing up.

"Hello," I answer.

"Look, nigga, don't try no funny shit. I want your bitch and I mean business! Oh, and don't look for me. You'll never find me. If you try anything funny, your mom is dead. I'll text you the information you need to bring the bitch to me. If you come on some bullshit, everybody dies. Got it?" King says.

"I ain't doing shit until I'm sure you'll release my mom!"

"Nigga, I'm making the rules to this shit. That bitch better be dead when I look out the peephole. I wanna see a body; if not, I'll give you your mother's body without her head," King said before ending the call.

I am trying to find a way to keep both my mom and Storm alive. This nigga has my whole heart in his hands. I feel like I am losing my mind. What am I supposed to do? I call Storm.

"Hello," she answers.

"Hey, baby, I need you to catch the next flight back to Detroit. When you land, catch a cab to the Holiday Inn in Canton. Call me when you settle in so I know what room you're in," I tell her.

"Okay, baby; is everything okay?" she asks.

"Yes, things are good," I lie. Trying to fight back tears, I end the call. I text my mom's phone to let King know I'll see him soon. My time is running out and I need to get my mother back safe. The thought of the two women I love getting hurt makes me weak, and I begin to throw up. My nerves are bad. I can't trust my boys and I really need a plan to keep Storm alive. Stone is all I have and he isn't in his right mind. His answer to everything is killing everybody.

I sit in my car for hours. I don't know how to pull this off. I am so hurt inside—how do I choose who gets to live? No one comes before my mom. I have no choice but to do what King has asked me to do. After we make that run east, Stone makes some moves. He calls my phone ten times until I answer.

"Hello," I answer.

"What's the word, kid?" Stone asked.

"Man, what am I supposed to do? I am almost out of time. I told Storm to catch a plane to the D—"

Before I can finish my sentence, Stone interrupts me. "Nigga, I *know* you ain't thinking about killing her!"

"Naw, man! I really ain't thinking about shit but my mom. If push comes to shove, Stone, I gotta go get my mom. What would you do if you were me?" I ask.

"Nigga, I don't even know."

"Well, I think I'm all out of moves. I have to surrender one of my queens," I say.

"Damn, this shit just keeps getting worse! I can't tell you what to do, just know I've got your back. If you wanna tear the whole city up, we can do that. Just keep me posted. I'm on standby."

Stone is my day-one nigga and I know he is all I have. I get the call from Storm four hours later. She has arrived at the hotel and is ready for me to come see her. Damn, my life so fucked up!

Chapter 13 ✳ Broken Heart

I call Face as soon as I get settled in the hotel. I'm not really sure what's going on, but he just doesn't sound like himself. I am so happy to be back in the D; I really miss Face.

I haven't seen my sister either. I have so much I need to do. My sister was at Kia's homegoing, but I haven't seen or heard from her since. I've been dodging her. She really doesn't know the truth about all the shit I've gotten myself into. I talked to my mom and she took Kia's death as hard as I did. She knew Kia was all I had until I found my sister.

I have so many regrets and I can't blame anyone but myself. What the hell was I thinking? What the fuck have I become? Shit! I begin to unpack my things so I can get comfortable. I call Aleeah and talk to her for a while, and I tell her where I am. When she asks about Kia, I say I still have no clue why she was murdered. We talk for an hour, and she notices the sadness in my voice when I begin to cry.

"I don't wanna go on without my Kia. It's so hard. I've called her phone a thousand times just to hear her voice," I cry.

"Stop crying, sister. There are some things we'll never understand. Please know at this moment, whatever you need from me, I'm here. I can't make your pain go away, but I can make you laugh. I can be your shoulder to cry on. I am here, baby sis," Aleeah said.

"I know, sis. Thanks a lot. I love you," I say.

"I love you, too," she says back.

We end our call and I begin to wonder what's taking Face so long. I jump in the shower, get out, and put my sexy gear on. I am really in need of some good loving. I fall asleep waiting on Face. My phone is blowing up and I get the strangest call. This call changes my life forever. I sit on the edge of the bed and begin to think really hard. Not knowing who I can trust any more, I prepare myself for the worst. I call Aleeah to confirm something. She tells me it is so. We end the call.

A knock at the door makes me jump. I peek out the peephole and see it's Face. I pull myself together and open the door. Never taking my eyes off him, I back away.

"Hey, baby; what's wrong? You don't look happy to see me," I say as Face walks in.

"Hey, baby," he says, holding his arms open for a hug. His voice is all shaky and his eyes are bloodshot-red.

"Face, what's going on? I know you, and you don't look so good," I say.

Face can't look me in my eyes. "Baby, that nigga King's got my mom."

"Let me guess, he wants me in exchange for her." I back away from Face and tears begin to fill my eyes. I can't believe he's here to hurt me.

"Baby, please don't cry. I love you. There are so many things I wish we could redo," Face says before I cut him off.

"Are you here to kill me, Face?" Please tell me you aren't that fuckin' dumb. Why would they spare her life? They hate you,

fool! Once I'm dead, they'll kill her to. How stupid could you be?"
I cry.

"Baby, it's my mom; I gotta save her. She had nothing to do with
the mess we created. This is going to be the hardest thing to do.
Come here, Storm. Can I please have one last kiss?"

Face stands in front of me with his arms open wide, crying like a
baby. He motions for me to come to him.

"Really, Face? I put my life on the line for you. I murdered that
nigga for you and this is the fuckin' thanks I get?! Now you want
me to come lie in your arms so you can blow my fuckin' head off?
My best friend is dead because of this shit. Now it's my turn? And
you and your old-ass mother get to skip away, hand-in-hand. I
thought you knew me, Face," I say.

"What do you mean? I do know you. I'm sorry it has come to this.
My mom is innocent. I gotta do what's right by her!" Face cries.

"KIA WAS INNOCENT. WHAT THE FUCK, FACE?!"

I pull my cellphone out of my robe pocket and place it on the
dresser. I call my voicemail and put the phone on speaker. The
voice on the phone says, "Hey, Storm, I don't have time to talk.
Wherever you are, please get your things and leave. Face is on his
way to you. He's coming to kill you."

"Do you recognize that voice?"

Face has a funny look on his face. He starts reaching for his gun.
I pull my gun quickly from my bra and point it at his head. With
tears rolling down my face, I say to the only man I've ever loved,
"You gotta be quicker than that. Now put your fuckin' hands
where I can see them before I blow your fuckin' head off!"

I press play again on my phone. That same voice said, "Storm, I know where I know you from. I was looking through some pictures I found at your house. I saw a picture of you and my mother. If your name is Reagan, you're my little sister. I'm not lying to you. My name is Marquest. I changed it to Mark years ago. I got the nickname Stone from Face when we were young and it just stuck. You were six when I left. Please trust me, little sis. Call me. I need to come get you."

Crying, I look at Face and say, "Good for me my long lost brother is your best friend. Too bad for you. Thank God he was going through pictures or I would be one dead bitch, huh?"

"Baby, let's talk. I love you. Give me a chance to explain," Face cries.

"Explain? Explain what? That you were going to take my life. Nigga, I killed for you. I'm sure you know that was all love. I love you, Face. So sorry I had to learn the hard way—when it comes to these streets, show no love because love will get you killed!" I cry.

"What are you saying?" Face asks.

"Love will never get me killed, because love doesn't live here anymore. I did all this shit for you. I'm glad I fucked Marko; hell, that was the only good thing I got out of this whole ordeal!" I say with a smirk on my face.

I put my finger on the trigger. Face nose flares up like a pit bull. I know he is ready to kill me at this point. "YOU BITCH! I KNEW YOUR ASS WAS OVER THERE GETTING DICKED. FUCK YOU, STORM! KILL ME, BITCH! PLEASE DO. SHIT, MY ASS IS ALREADY DEAD!" Face yells, crying like a baby.

My tears roll down my face like a waterfall. Looking at the man I love, knowing I will never see him again, hurts my heart. We stand there face-to-face in puddles of our own tears. My heart is pounding; my body shaking as we cry together, then I put a bullet in the front of his skull. It seems to happen in slow motion when his body begins to fall. My heart jumps out my chest and lands on his dying body. I've killed the only man I've ever loved, because I killed to protect him. I lean down over Face's body.

"One last kiss," I whisper before I kiss him on his bloody lips.

I have all my things ready to go. I change my clothes, put them in a bag in my luggage, wipe down the room, and put the 'Do Not Disturb' sign on the door. I walk to the lobby, trying to look as normal as possible, but my body is shaking and I've left my heart lying dead on the hotel floor. I go outside and flag down a cab. I text the number Stone left on my voice mail and tell him to meet me at the airport. I have to make it seem like I've just got off the plane.

When I pull up Stone is waiting on me. I run to him and fall into his arms. For more than one reason, I cry like a baby. Stone drops a few tears as well. Just seeing me alive, lets him know his best friend is dead. We jump in his truck and pull off.

"You know it's time to end this war," Stone says.

I nod my head yeah. I grab Face's cell phone from my pocket and text the number King left. *I have her. She's dead. Where's my mom?*

He replies. *Bring her to me and I'll set your mom free.*

I text back. *I need to hear my mom's voice.*

The phone rings and I pass it to Stone. He tries his best to sound like Face. "Hello."

"Hey, baby, I'm okay," Face's mother says and ends the call.

Stone passes the cell phone back to me. "Well, what do you think?" I ask.

"Now he's going to kill her."

I just look out the window. My heart is completely broken. One stupid-ass decision causes three murders and I am sure there are more to come. Tears roll down my face as I think back on all the good times we had together. I keep seeing the moments where Stone and I were trying to figure out how we knew each other. I think of the day my sister asked who Stone was. She also said he looked familiar, but she'd only seen him from the side. I laughed; he's been with me all along.

"It's okay, little sis. I ain't gon let anyone hurt you again," Stone says as he rubs my back. Stone makes a couple of calls. "Look, sis, I've got some heavy hitters who owe me big time. They'll be coming with us. We're about to knock these fools off."

I just nod my head. I feel like shit. I can get the vision of Face's body hitting the floor out of my mind. We arrive at the spot to meet these hitters Stone is so sure of. The plan is for me to be carried to the door. I change back into my already-bloody clothes from lying on Face's dead body; all I have to do is look dead. Once the door is open, Stone's crew will ambush King and his crew.

Stone texts King and gets the address where he is to make the drop. I mess my hair up and wet the side so it looks like I have a wound to the head. We pull up and Stone carries me to the door. I swear there are at least fifteen niggas with us. I have my gun tucked in my waistband. Stone does the special knock.

When King opens the door, Stone rolls me on to the floor and I end up facedown. I have my hand under my shirt, on my gun. I am ready to kill the nigga who killed my best friend. I hear Stone yell "MOVE" which is my signal to start busting. I roll over as gunfire comes from all directions. Stone's boys rush in and it's on.

I see King and Stone going head up. I start shooting at King and I get his ass in the back. I crawl behind the sofa to take cover. Stone is right: Face's mom is on the floor, dead, with a gunshot to the back of her head. I lie behind the couch, right next to her body. Tears roll down my face. I have to let this shit go. My life is on the line and I have to fight for it.

"STORM! STORM!" Stone calls out to me. "IT'S CLEAR."

Just as I begin to come up to run out, I hear one last gunshot. In slow motion, I see Stone hit the floor. As I run over to him, I notice King isn't dead. I stand over him and shoot him dead in his head. I begin to scream. "NO! NO! NO!" as Stone's boy picks me up and carries me out the door. "MY BROTHER! GET MY BROTHER," I yell. Mike throws me in the car and pulls off.

As we leave, I see Nutty carrying Stone's body out the building. I am so worried about Stone as Mike drives me to an unknown location. I cry the whole time. I can't believe Stone is my brother. Nutty takes Stone to the hospital; I don't know his status. All I know is he was hit in the chest because Nutty told us. Nutty says he told the police they were walking past the apartments, a shootout started, and that's how Stone got hit. Stone is in surgery for hours. Doctors aren't sure if he will survive. All we can do is pray.

Damn, this little life of mine . . .

A New Start

"Today we will be going over the different types of trials. If you have your assignment from yesterday, please pass it forward," Mr. Kindle says to the class.

"Reagan are you ready for your big speech tomorrow?' he asks me.

"Yes, sir, I'm ready," I say to my favorite teacher.

The time has come for me to graduate college. I am getting my masters in Criminal Justice. Graduating with honors, I am very proud of myself. Funny ain't it? I was asked to speak to Mr. Kindle's class today to prepare me for tomorrow. Mr. Kindle adores me. He says I am too smart for my own good.

I like to think Kia is helping me with my work. I talk to her ashes that are still hanging around my neck. For some strange reason, whenever I do so, I get an 'A' on my assignment. I miss my friend so much. I've tried my best to live my life looking ahead, realizing my past made me who I am. I do my speech and it goes really well. Mr. Kindle says he knew I would do great. I go home and get some much-needed rest.

The day has come for me to walk in my cap and gown. I am so happy, I can't stop smiling.

"Girl, sit your fidgety self still and let me finish your hair," Aleeah says to me as she puts my cap on. She has done my makeup and picked my outfit for the day. I stand up and look in the mirror.

"You look beautiful, baby," Mom says as she enters the room. "I am so proud of you. I may have missed your other graduations, but this one means so much more to me for some reason."

"It's time to go, lil sis," Aleeah says. My mom kisses me and we walk out.

The ceremony is beautiful. When I finish my speech, the crowd goes wild. The best part is seeing all of my family together— Mom, Aleeah, Mario, Maurice, and Mark a.k.a. Stone. Yup, my brother made it through and this is the happiest day of my life.

Stone was on life support for six months. Once he was off, he did six months of therapy. Mom came home and took over like she'd never left. We were all like babies again. Our childhood wasn't great but mom tries her best to make us forget our pasts. Aleeah's husband had two houses built in Las Vegas, side-by-side. The boys and I share a house with Mom. Aleeah and her husband live next door. We moved as far away from the Detroit as we could.

Things have been great. My brothers are all working and living life on the positive side. Aleeah is still a stay-at-home wife, but she's the best wife in the world to me. I have struggled with my life and my past. It's hard to move on when all you've done has been bad.

I still love Face and I forgive him for his decision to kill me over his mom. I love my mom and would do anything for her, so I really do understand. I will *never* forget Face. He's the first man I ever loved. He taught me so much. Even moments before I killed him, he taught me that love don't love nobody. I thought Face would love me 'til death. Well, I guess he did. Too bad he ended up being my *Koldest Kill.*

Now I lay me down to sleep
I pray the Lord my soul to keep
If I should die before I wake
I pray the Lord my soul to take

Forgive me, Father, for I have sinned
Please keep in my heart my dearest friend
Keep me, Father, I wish to do your will
Protect my heart, mind, and soul
So thy shall not kill

Also available by Silver Ray . . .

In Real Life: A True Story

My life had been a rollercoaster ever since I met Drew. It started off good and fun, but ended up bad and sad. I asked God all the time, "Why me? What did I do to deserve so much pain?" I haven't received an answer yet. My husband has been gone for six months now. I've received one letter and that's it. He'd become so down and depressed that he refused to have contact with the outside world. I sent letters almost every other day and never received a response. I would call up to the prison and ask questions about Blake; they would tell me that he was there and he was fine. All I knew was that my husband was still breathing. My heart hurt so badly.

My children didn't understand why Daddy had just up and left. I told them he was on vacation. I'd kept my shop and Blake's carwash going, so I was doing really well financially, but emotionally I was beat down. I was lonely and angry all the time. The only thing that kept me going was the love I have for my children. I promised myself that I wouldn't let anybody come between my family, and I meant that.

Although Blake wasn't keeping in touch, he was still my husband. I remained faithful and stayed to myself. I wasn't happy, but I was okay. What else could I do but be okay? All of my girls had my back. They kept me company a lot so I wouldn't be down. Money and Shorty brought their children over to play with mine. We raised them as cousins.

One day, I needed to get out so I had Money keep the children so I could go shopping at the mall. I had to get out of my little box. I went to my favorite mall, Fairlane, and shopped 'til I was ready to drop. I had so many bags that I had to go take them to my car then go back in the mall. I went in one more store before I decided that my shopping spree was over. As I walked into the Diamond Hut, my phone began to ring. I was so busy looking in my purse as I entered the store that I bumped into someone. I answered but I couldn't respond to the person on the phone; I was shocked and scared of what I had just seen. I wiped my scared expression off my face and turned to walk back out the store.

A huge hand grabbed my shoulder and a deep voice said, "Rocky, I'm not going to hurt you. It's good to see you."

The look on my face said it all. I was scared as hell. It was Drew. Although I hadn't seen him in four years, the fear he'd left in my heart was still there.

"Hi, Drew; how are you?" I asked with a shaky voice.

"I'm fine. You look great. I heard you're married with children now?" Drew smiled.

"Yes, that's true; I am. How about yourself?"

My heart was pounding so badly that I couldn't hear Drew's response. I was ready to go and didn't know how to end the conversation. As my mind raced and my heart skipped beats, a young woman came over and told Drew she was ready to leave. I said to myself, "Thank God for her." She gave me a funny look, and I smiled as I walked off. I never looked back. That shit was weird and scary at the same time. Life is a trip. It throws all kind of curveballs at you when you're not looking. My day was just about over. As I left the mall, I looked around the parking lot to make sure I wasn't being followed. I jumped in my truck and pulled off. For the most part, I'd had a relaxing day. I picked up my girls and we headed home.

৯০৫

The next morning when I got up, I got ready for work, got my girls dressed, and we had our breakfast. We packed our bags and headed for the door. Just as I stepped my foot out on the porch, my home phone rang. Something told me to answer it, but I said, "Fuck it; if it's important, they'll call my cell phone." I dropped the girls off at daycare and headed to the shop.

When I arrived at the shop, there was a basketful of yellow roses and rose petals. The card was blank. I couldn't get my thoughts together. My heart was racing and I couldn't catch my breath. I asked my receptionist who dropped the basket off. She said a tall, dark-skinned man. I looked around outside to see if he was still around. Blake had always sent me yellow roses, but everybody knew how he looked, and I knew it wasn't him. I put the box on my station and worked all day, wondering who had sent the box. I called my girls and told them about my strange day. We all tripped out for a while then ended our phone call. I cleaned up my shop and headed home.

When I got home, I took a shower and changed into something cute and comfortable. I lit some candles and turned on some slow jams. I poured a sip of wine and lay on my chaise. As I began to doze off, I was awakened by a soft kiss on the forehead. When I opened my eyes, it was Blake holding a yellow rose and a box of jewelry. I cried as I jumped up and grabbed for him. I just couldn't get a grip, and I started to cry harder.

"Baby, I love you. I love you and I've missed you so much," I said as I cried louder.

"I love you, too," Blake said as the image of him faded away.

I woke up in a cold sweat with tears running down my face. It was only a dream. My husband wasn't back and I was still alone.

I got up and walked into my girls' bedroom. They were sound asleep as I kissed them both.

"I love you, my sweet girls."

My tears covered their faces. My heart hurt for them as well as for myself. The man we all knew and loved was gone. We had to deal with it until the day their father, my friend, my husband returned. This was it . . . In Real Life.

61026514R00079

Made in the USA
Lexington, KY
26 February 2017